THE ROCK SLAB SHIFTED.

Kirk peeled himself off the slab, pulling Reinhart with him. Then the doorway slid up, revealing the passageway into the station.

Kirk straightened his uniform. "An effective system, I'm sure Mr. Spock would say."

"Yes, sir," Reinhart said, in obvious relief.

As they reentered the main chamber, Spock glanced down. "Any trouble, Captain?"

"None, Mr. Spock."

Reinhart took a deep breath. Whatever he had been about to say was lost in his shout: "Watch out! She's back!"

The humming came from the wall behind Kirk, where Losira appeared.

STAR TREK®
GATEWAYS
BOOK ONE OF SEVEN

ONE SMALL STEP

Susan Wright

Based upon STAR TREK®
created by Gene Roddenberry

POCKET BOOKS
New York   London   Toronto   Sydney   Singapore

An *Original* Publication of POCKET BOOKS

 POCKET BOOKS, a division of Simon & Schuster, Inc.
1230 Avenue of the Americas, New York, NY 10020

Copyright © 2001 by Paramount Pictures. All Rights Reserved.

STAR TREK is a Registered Trademark of Paramount Pictures.

A VIACOM COMPANY

This book is published by Pocket Books, a division of Simon & Schuster, Inc., under exclusive license from Paramount Pictures.

ISBN: 0-7434-1854-9

First Pocket Books printing August 2001

10 9 8 7 6 5 4 3 2 1

POCKET and colophon are registered trademarks of Simon & Schuster, Inc.

Printed in the U.S.A.

Prologue

COMMANDER LOSIRA DISAPPEARED. Her body compressed into a thick line before vanishing in a flash of light.

Captain James T. Kirk was touched by the expression of profound sorrow on her face. Despite the lack of life-form readings, he was certain this woman was not an android.

His last question had been *"Are you lonely?"* For certainly her attitude supported her claim that the others on this station were "no more." But she hadn't answered him.

"She must be somewhere!" Lt. Sulu exclaimed.

McCoy was busy with his tricorder. "She's not registering."

"Then there's another power surge." Captain Kirk examined the readings on the tricorder Sulu had given him. "Off the scale, like a door closing. It must be near here."

Kirk and his landing party had been stranded for one day on this strange planetoid, and they were being forced to defend their lives. Losira was capable of killing with a single touch, yet she appeared to loathe doing it.

Though Kirk had appealed to Losira, questioning her desire to kill when she knew it was wrong, she had continued to try to touch him. The fact that she was beautiful, with a haunting pain in her eyes, made it even worse.

The lovely killer had already murdered Senior Geologist D'Amato, a member of the landing party. D'Amato had been a gifted scientist and a fine officer. Kirk felt his loss as only a commander could.

Kirk was also concerned about Ensign Wyatt, who had been manning the transporter as the landing party beamed down to the planetoid. Losira had somehow bypassed security on the *Enterprise* and had appeared in the transporter room just as the landing party dematerialized. There was no telling what she had done to Wyatt or the rest of his crew. Losira had significantly damaged Mr. Sulu's shoulder with only a glancing brush of her fingertips.

Everything would be different if only the *Enterprise*—his ship!—had not disappeared. There was nothing: no radiation, no wreckage near the rogue planetoid. His ship was simply gone.

Kirk refused to believe that the *Enterprise* had been destroyed during that first enormous power surge that had shaken the planetoid. He would not fear the worst.

The key to their survival was Losira. What kind of alien was she? At the very least, someone to be treated with extreme caution.

That didn't stop Kirk from tracking the source of the magnetic sweep they had detected. The high-pitched whine of the tricorder was the only sound as he followed the residual energy readings, circling several large rock outcroppings to trace the path of the energy waves.

He didn't have to order Dr. McCoy and Lieutenant Sulu to follow. Sulu was still suffering from the wound Losira had inflicted on him, but except for a slight breathlessness, he was doing a good job of hiding the pain from his superior officers.

As they followed the search pattern, McCoy asked, "Is the power level still holding, Jim?"

"Right off the scale." Kirk glanced up as he stepped around a clump of yellow and blue grass sprinkled with tiny red flowers. "It's remained at a peak ever since Losira disappeared."

Kirk kept walking, noting that the proximity locator was approaching 0 degrees. Yet this area looked no different from the rest of the rock-strewn land they had already passed. Many of the outcroppings appeared to have been deliberately tortured into looming shapes. In the distance, cutting off the horizon, were spiky, black hills.

The landing party had recently discovered that the topsoil was only a thin layer, covering a red-colored shell of diburnium-osmium alloy. Kirk thought the manufactured planetoid was singularly ugly, except for the sparkling minerals in the greenish-gray rocks that cast off silver, gold, and blue flickers whenever he moved.

The sky was a permanent, threatening purplish-pink, completely unlike its appearance from space. The view from onboard his ship had been of a typical class-M atmosphere, with a white cloud-filled sky over blue water. They still had not determined what created the surface light, since the planetoid was not in orbit around any sun. They had found no trace of water on the surface.

The lack of a sun made the spindly blue and yellow blades of grass all the more perplexing. Most of the vegetation seemed dry. Kirk was not surprised that the plants were poisonous to humans, even the bright red flowers, which were the most compelling foliage he had seen here.

Concentrating on the tricorder, Kirk approached the massive gray butte that towered above them. It looked like solid rock, nothing unusual about it.

"The entrance is . . ." Kirk turned nearly in a circle until the indicator was on zero. "Here!"

The entire rock slab shifted, making Kirk look up. A thick ledge slid aside, belying its bulk, and revealed a red door in the rock behind. This door slid up to reveal a narrow passageway, lit by a faint, green glow.

Kirk half-expected Losira to appear in the doorway, but nothing happened. They stood in silence for a moment, peering inside.

"You think we're being invited in?" McCoy drawled.

"It certainly looks like it," Kirk agreed. "And the invitation doesn't exactly relax me."

Sulu finally spoke up. "I'd rather be on the *Enterprise,* sir."

"I agree."

"We've been led here," McCoy said. "Why?"

"I don't know. But whatever civilization exists on this planet is in there." Kirk pointed toward the open doorway. "And without the *Enterprise,* gentlemen, the only source of food and water is also in there. Let's go."

Taking the lead, Kirk went through the doorway. The narrow rough-walled passageway slanted steeply downward, then curved in a U-shape, taking them back in the direction they had come, descending even lower.

Finally they stepped into a large, ovoid chamber. The walls were smoothed to a polished shine, supported by discrete alloy beams every few meters. The lights tinted everything as pink as the sky outside, including the ceiling, which had been left rough-hewn bluish rock.

A large white cube had been set into the center of the ceiling, directly above their heads. The cube pulsed in a mesmerizing flow of colors. It reflected an iridescent light against the walls of the chamber and across the faces of Dr. McCoy and Mr. Sulu.

Kirk took one step forward, aiming the tricorder at the cube. His first thought was that the cube housed the computer that operated this place.

Suddenly, a black, vertical line appeared underneath the cube. The line expanded sideways to reveal Losira. Her glossy, dark hair was rolled away from her face and gathered in the back to fall down to her shoulders. Her eyes and dark brows slanted upward at the outer corners, highlighted by green and pink streaks on her eyelids. Her uniform was unusual—a purple two-piece, edged with silver braid. The cap sleeves and collar were attached to a narrow bodice. The pants had a square flap covering her bare stomach, suspended by nothing that Kirk could see.

Losira's anguished expression did not match her determined step forward. One hand raised.

"Who have you come for?" Kirk demanded.

This time, she didn't reply. Perhaps she had learned better from their last encounter, when the landing party had successfully kept her from touching him. Now her eyes shifted to look at each of them as her steps quickened. She spread both hands wide, preparing to touch any one of them.

The *Enterprise* officers backed away slightly.

"Form a circle," Kirk ordered.

Losira halted, momentarily confused as the three men surrounded her. Slowly they circled her, staying just out of reach, taunting her to see which one she would choose.

Kirk knew they had her now. "You see, you'd better tell us." He shifted to her right as McCoy took his place. "Tell us . . . who have you come for?"

McCoy was too close, and though Losira could have touched him, she didn't. Instead, she seemed to always keep an eye on Kirk.

"You're a very determined woman. For me?"

"I am for James T. Kirk," she agreed sadly.

"Gentlemen!" Kirk called out. "I'll need your help."

McCoy and Sulu leaped together in front of the captain, blocking Losira.

"Please . . . I must touch you. I beg it," she pleaded, one hand held out toward him despite the intervening men. "It is my existence."

"We have seen the results of your touch." Kirk held his place behind McCoy and Sulu.

"But you are my match, James Kirk." Her insistence was almost painful. "I *must* touch you. Then I will live as one, even to the structure of your cells and the arrangement of chromosomes. I need you."

"That is how you kill," Kirk insisted. She stepped forward, as if to push her way through McCoy and Sulu. "You will never reach me."

Even as he spoke, a second woman appeared. She was identical to Losira. She silently moved toward them.

"Watch out!" Kirk exclaimed.

The second Losira said, "I am for McCoy." Her pose was identical to the first Losira.

Kirk moved to block the doctor from her. "That computer! It must be programming these replicas."

"The women match our chromosome patterns after they touch us," McCoy agreed.

Sulu quickly added, "It's a very painful affair, I can tell you!"

Suddenly, a third Losira appeared. They looked identical, from their clothing to their exquisite, tormented faces.

"I am for Sulu," the third Losira replica announced.

"Shift positions!" Kirk ordered.

They moved quickly, so they each faced a Losira replica that wasn't meant for them. Kirk glanced from his men to the replicas, instantly rejecting impossible defenses. They were defenseless in this echoing chamber, empty except for the computer cube overhead.

"Captain, we can no longer protect each other!" Sulu cried out.

Silently, the three identical replicas approached, their hands outstretched and their faces resolute. They moved in, closer and closer, as the three *Enterprise* men drew together.

Behind the replicas, the air began to shimmer. Kirk felt the familiar distortion of a transporter beam at close range.

Mr. Spock and an *Enterprise* security guard materialized behind the Losira replicas. They were both armed with phasers.

Spock and the security guard looked first at the threatening women, but Kirk yelled, "Spock! That cubed computer—destroy it!"

The blue beam from the security guard's phaser hit the pulsing cube, causing vivid red sparks. Kirk finally noticed a subliminal sound when it began to falter as the iridescent colors slowed and began to move sluggishly. The cube dimmed and actually seemed to grow smaller as the light ceased to blaze through the chamber.

The three replicas disappeared.

McCoy gasped in relief, supporting Mr. Sulu, who staggered slightly.

Kirk turned to Spock, his first thought for the *Enterprise*. His ship must be safe, or Spock wouldn't be here.

"Mr. Spock!" Kirk shook his head, almost laughing in relief at such a close call. "I certainly am glad to see you. I thought you and the *Enterprise* had been destroyed."

His Vulcan first officer appeared exactly the same as when Kirk had left him in charge of the bridge yesterday. "I had the same misgivings about you, Captain. We returned and picked up your life-form readings only a moment ago."

Kirk asked, "Returned from where?"

Spock stepped closer to the computer cube, looking up at it in admiration. Kirk wasn't surprised, joining him underneath to be sure it wasn't still a threat. The colors were hardly moving anymore, barely showing life. Otherwise, the exterior shell appeared unharmed.

"From where this brain had the power to send the *Enterprise* . . . nine-hundred-and-ninety point seven light-years across the galaxy. What a remarkable culture this is."

"*Was,* Mr. Spock. Its defenses were run by computer."

Spock nodded. "I surmised that, Captain. Its moves were immensely logical." Spock glanced around the polished chamber. "But what people created this? Are there any representatives here?"

"There *were* replicas of one of them." Kirk thought of Losira and her distress over her need to kill them. "But the power to re-create them has been destroyed."

"*That* is a loss, Captain," Spock said flatly.

"Well, you wouldn't have thought so, Mr. Spock, if you had been among us."

A low humming distracted the captain. Turning, he saw a distortion on the blank wall of the chamber behind them.

Losira's image gradually formed. It was different from the replicas, reflected flat on the wall, and showed her only from the knees up. Her lips opened briefly in a slight smile.

"*My fellow Kalandans, welcome. A disease has destroyed us. Beware of it. After your long journey, I'm sorry to give you only a recorded welcome. But we who have guarded the station for you will be dead by the time you take possession of this planet.*"

Her voice faltered for a moment, then resumed.

"*I am the last of our advance force left alive. Too late, our physicians discovered the cause of this sickness that killed us. In creating this planet, we have accidentally created a deadly organism. I have awaited the regular supply ship from our home star with medical assistance, but . . . I doubt now they will arrive in time. I shall set the station's controls on automatic. The computer will selectively defend against all life-forms except our own. My fellow Kalandans—I, Losira, wish you well."*

Her image remained on the wall, but her eyes closed as if to indicate that she was through fighting to keep them open.

McCoy looked glum. "The previous ships probably spread the disease right through their people. The supply ship she was waiting for never came. All these thousands of years, she's been waiting to greet people who were . . . dead."

Spock's eyes returned to the still computer cube. "To do the job of defense, the computer projected a replica of the only image available—Losira's."

Kirk's eyes remained on the impassive image of Losira, who continued to stand with her eyes closed. "The computer was too perfect. It projected so much of Losira's personality into the replica that it felt regret—guilt—at killing. That bought us the time we needed to destroy it." He paused, looking at Losira. "She must have been a remarkable woman."

"And beautiful!" McCoy exclaimed.

Spock briefly shook his head. "Beauty is transitory, Doctor. However she was, evidently, highly intelligent."

The image of Losira on the wall disappeared, leaving them alone in the echoing chamber. No Kalandans would ever walk here again. Kirk felt strangely let down.

The captain flipped open his communicator. "Kirk to *Enterprise*. Five of us to beam up." He waited for confirmation. "I don't agree with you, Mr. Spock."

"Indeed, Captain?"

Kirk remembered Losira's voice, melodic and soothing. And her lovely face, flinching in horror at the idea of killing him. It was heartrending to think of Losira waiting in vain for the return of her people, and salvation.

There was too much to say. All he could manage was, "Beauty . . . survives."

Spock stared at him for a moment. There was a small, sad smile on Kirk's lips. He knew he could never explain it to his first officer.

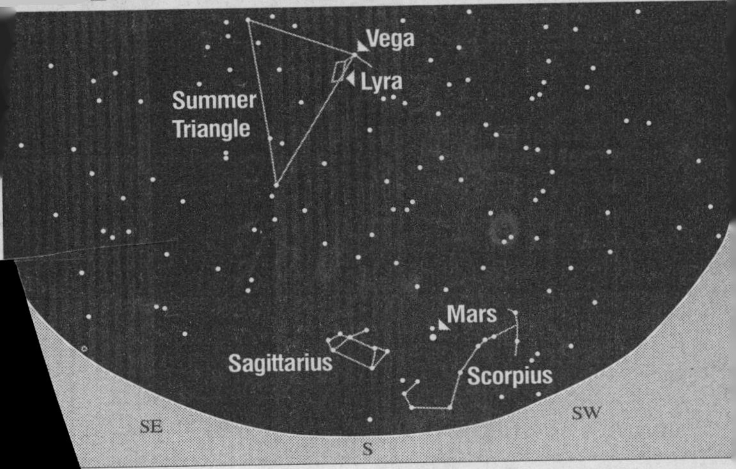

Summer
Triangle

Sagittarius

Vega
Lyra

Mars

Scorpius

SE

S

SW

Soundir
on airbag

Auto crashes occur in seconds, but, in that time, a lot happens. Typically, tires screech, riders gasp and brace themselves as best they can, and there's the awful metallic thud of impact.

But it's another

**WHEEL
WOMAN**

Chapter One

DR. MCCOY JOINED the captain and Spock to prepare for transport. The transporter wasn't one of his favorite pieces of technology, but this time he was almost eager to be split into a billion bits. Anything to get off this blighted dustball and back to civilization.

He had been forced to sleep in the dirt last night, but at least he had been on top of it rather than under a tomb of rocks, like Senior Geologist D'Amato. Their rescue had been close—none of the landing party had had a sip of water for nearly twenty-four hours. He, for one, was ready for a hot meal and a long sonic shower.

Sulu also took his position in the proscribed circle for transport. He was holding his arm again, in pain from the injured shoulder. Dehydration had aggravated the wound.

McCoy tensed, anticipating the familiar tug of the transporter.

The chamber seemed to sparkle and fade. But it was

only for a moment. Then they were back again, inside the Kalandan station.

"The joys of modern technology!" McCoy exclaimed. "How can anyone trust these things?"

Kirk flipped his communicator open. *"Enterprise, what happened?"*

"Sir!" The voice of the transporter operator wavered. *"The automatic sequence was interrupted by a biofilter alert. There is an unknown organism in your systems."*

McCoy unslung his medical tricorder. "It must be the organism that the Kalandans accidentally created."

Spock also began to scan the chamber. Security Guard Joe Reinhart, a big, stocky man, looked distinctly uncomfortable.

Pulling out the tiny medical scanner, McCoy checked Reinhart. "Go ahead and breathe. It's already infected all of us."

"Fascinating," Spock murmured. "There are several unusual parasites on this planetoid."

"The one inside us doesn't appear to be a true virus, but it's certainly not bacterial." McCoy shook his head over his medical scanner. "This thing can't seem to pinpoint the exact nature of the organism."

Kirk nodded shortly. "That must be why the transporter biofilter didn't work."

"I'll have to perform a level one bio-scan," McCoy agreed. "That will give the computer the specifications it needs."

Sulu was looking bleak. "That could take hours."

Kirk glanced around the chamber, placing his fists on his hips. "Gentlemen, it looks like we'll be here for a while longer. Might as well make ourselves comfortable."

McCoy grumbled, "Sure, *you* get comfortable while I get to work."

"Aren't doctors always on call?" The captain adjusted the dial on his communicator. "Kirk to *Enterprise.* No one, I repeat, no one is to transport down to the station until further orders."

Scotty sounded determined. *"Aye, sir. I wish Wyatt was here. He was a genius with biofiltration systems. I'll just run down—"*

"Hold on there, Scotty. What happened to Wyatt?" Kirk glanced at Spock, who was nodding slowly.

"I'm sorry, Captain, Transporter Chief Wyatt was killed at his station."

Kirk clenched his jaw while McCoy felt his stomach twist. None of them had wanted to believe the transporter chief was dead. Wyatt had been seeing one of McCoy's nurses for the past year. Medical Technician Michaels must be distraught right now.

Security Guard Reinhart was looking uncomfortable. "We never found the intruder who killed Wyatt or Engineer Watkins."

"Watkins, too?" Kirk demanded. Now he looked angry. "How?"

Scotty must have thought the question was directed at him. *"According to Dr. M'Benga's autopsy, Captain, every cell in their bodies was disrupted. We don' know how it happened, but I heard Watkins call out a warning about a woman in engineering."*

"Could it have been Losira?" Sulu asked, startled.

"I don't doubt it," Kirk said flatly.

That made three crew members dead. McCoy sincerely hoped they would be the last, but he had a feeling it wouldn't be that easy.

Scotty was saying, *"I ran to help, Captain, but I dinna get there in time."*

"It's not your fault, Scotty. None of us could stop her."

"Aye, Captain." Scotty sounded unconvinced.

"Maintain an open channel to sickbay so Dr. McCoy can perform a level one bio-scan."

"That we can do, Captain."

"And Scotty, perform a continuous scan of this sector for approaching ships. Since this is unexplored territory, there's no telling who might happen by."

"Aye," Scotty agreed dourly. *"We'll keep an eye out up here. Don' you worry about that."*

McCoy half-listened while Spock continued briefing Kirk on what had happened while the landing party was stranded. The captain only interrupted once to express shock at the extreme warp speed the *Enterprise* had managed to sustain. What would normally take months to travel at warp 9, had taken little more than a day at warp 14. It was typical of Spock to act like it was all in a normal day's work.

Meanwhile, McCoy started sending orders to Dr. M'Benga in sickbay. Not only did he order a portable bio-computer and diagnostic unit, but he also asked the technicians to send down half-a-dozen emergency ration kits, complete with food and water. It wasn't as good as a sonic shower, but with a little bit of nourishment inside him, he could tackle this organism and get them back to the ship before the next duty-shift.

Near the Starfleet border, the cruiser *'Ong* of the Klingon Defense Force made its scheduled rounds.

Captain Mox had been spending most of his time in his own narrow quarters. Only Mox knew why, but his crew would find out soon enough. Any time now, one of his officers would receive tidings from Qo'noS containing the latest news of his father, Sowron.

As a devoted follower of the Cult of Kahless, Mox believed in honor above all. Kahless had shown the way, decreeing that a warrior's honor was founded on the honor of his father's house. And Mox's father had no honor!

Mox slammed his fist into the reinforced wall above his sleep bench. There was a sour stench in the air from his unwashed, unkempt body. For days he had battered the walls of his chamber, to no avail. He kept the lights low, so the heavy bulkheads curved into the darkness over his head. He wanted no witness to his struggle, not even himself.

His crew would never understand. He was the only one on board who adhered to Kahless' teachings. Some of his crew complained about his strict adherence to honor. Their scorn would flow freely when they found out about his father. Many would doubtless be amused that Sowron had squandered the family fortune on attempted "cures" after he had fallen sick with a wasting illness. Then Sowron had fallen down dead in the City Council Chamber in front of gathered officials from across the Klingon Empire, struck down by a tiny parasite that had slowly eaten away his gut.

Mox let out a roar of fury every time he thought of it. He would not return for his father's funeral. His father was nothing to him now.

He could find no resolution, as much as he tore at his armor and hair, growling in frustration. If only he could go to battle! Only *that* would restore honor to his family.

No—if only his father had listened to the words of

Kahless! A true Klingon would have ended his life in glory, choosing a valiant enemy to battle his way to death. But no, not his father. From a mighty house, they had fallen far.

Mox was in the foulest of tempers when his first officer signaled. Gulda's surly face was the same as usual, her frizzy brown hair standing on end. *"Captain! Long-range sensors are picking up the remnants of a power surge. From the degradation of the signal, it appears that, at the source, the energy expended would have been off the scale."*

Mox called up the log on his screen without bothering to settle his bulk into the chair. "It comes from near Federation territory."

"Yes, Captain. Shall I relay the information to High Command?" There was an odd look in Gulda's eyes, no doubt taking in her captain's disheveled armor and his bleeding fists.

Mox made his decision. "Set course for the source of that power surge."

"But, Captain—" his first officer protested, her sneer becoming more pronounced.

"TammoH!" Mox shouted.

So Gulda knew. That meant they all knew.

She was sullen as Mox ordered, "Proceed at warp 8."

"By your command, Captain!" She did him the courtesy of waiting until Mox closed the channel first.

Mox knew his first officer would do as he said, but her slow response would show her disdain. His crew would mock his dishonor as surely as they had chafed under his rules.

All of his warriors would react like Gulda. But none would dare break rank and contact Klingon High Command about their course alteration. They were heading toward the furthest reaches of space, where the Neutral Zone had not yet been designated. It was one vast, unexplored zone, so, technically, Mox was not violating orders.

Before his dishonor, he would have been satisfied to report the unusual power surge to High Command. His duty rotation would have taken him out of the area before his superiors could determine whether they wanted the phenomenon investigated.

Now, it was in his hands. Mox intended to wrest some glory from this mission if it took every drop of blood in his body and that of his crew to do it. He would give his crew a chance to die a good and noble death. Whether they appreciated it or not.

While McCoy analyzed the bio-readings of the deadly organism, Spock took the opportunity to examine the computer cube. At his request, the *Enterprise* sent down a lift unit to raise him up to the crumpled rock ceiling of the chamber.

Getting the outer casing off proved to be a challenge, but one that Spock met with dispatch. The cube was attached to the ceiling with electrostatic bolts. With the muted colors still cycling over the surface, Spock laid the cube on one of the telescoping supports of the lift.

Inside the cube were hundreds of thousands of monofilaments connecting to various devices, which Spock proceeded to scan. The other ends of the monofilaments disappeared into a stasis-sealed junction in the rock ceiling.

Spock theorized that the cube was an interface node, operated by a computer in a remote location via the monofilaments. That theory was confirmed by the statements made by Losira in her message concerning the computer defense system. However, he was unable to trace the monofilaments beyond the edge of the wall, where they disappeared behind the diburnium-osmium alloy. Even the sensors on the *Enterprise* weren't able to detect anything beneath the layer of diburnium and osmium. These alloys should not be capable of blocking their sensors, so Spock surmised that something else was contributing to the sensor block.

Due to McCoy's unfortunate habit of talking aloud while he worked, Spock was able to simultaneously follow the medical analysis while he performed his own investigation. The doctor evidently considered the organism to be a "near-virus." There were subatomic anomalies that McCoy couldn't explain, but the doctor repeatedly assured Captain Kirk that a basic identification should be enough for the transporter to filter the organisms out of their systems.

Spock was familiar with an antiquated human quote about protesting too much, but he refrained from comment.

McCoy downloaded his work and transmitted the specs of the organism to the ship's computer. "That should do it. Now the biofilter will be able to handle this bug."

Kirk jumped up, ready to go. Spock followed at a slower pace. He intended to return to the Kalandan station at his earliest convenience to continue his investigation.

"Prepare to transport," Kirk ordered.

The five crew members stood in a circle, anticipating transport. The degree of muscular tension in Kirk's stance indicated that he was impatient to return to the *Enterprise*. He was naturally concerned about the damage done to the ship by Losira's sabotage. Power overloads and malfunctions had occurred in almost every system. The fused matter/antimatter integrator had severely damaged the warp engines. At the time of the crisis, Spock had estimated their chances of survival were a mere twelve percent. However, Mr. Scott had performed his job adequately, and the engines were shut down by a manual bypass of the integrator.

"Energize," Kirk ordered into the communicator.

There was a brief disorientation as dematerialization began. But the cycle ceased 1.204 seconds into the sequence. The landing party remained on the Kalandan station.

"What in blue blazes *is* this thing!" McCoy exploded.

"I don't know, Doctor, but it's *your* job to find out." Kirk adjusted his communicator. "Scotty, as you can see, it didn't work."

"Aye, Captain. There appears t' be a problem with the quantum differentials."

Kirk gave Dr. McCoy a sidelong glance. "We'll factor that into our calculations." Snapping the communicator closed, Kirk asked, "What's next, Doctor?"

"Well, I can't even tell if it's an organism that mimics a virus or the other way around," McCoy wearily admitted. "I'm not sure how we got infected, though it's most likely airborne, because it happened so quickly."

Spock ascertained that the doctor was paler than normal. Humans had a tendency to react adversely when deprived of their comforts, McCoy more so than others, in his opinion.

Susan Wright

Indeed, Kirk ordered, "Why don't you get some rest, Bones? Now that the ship has your specs on the organism, the medical staff can take over your analysis."

McCoy hardly protested before going to lie down next to Sulu, flinging one arm over his eyes to shield them from the bright ambient light.

Security Guard Reinhart was seated on the other side of the chamber, keeping watch on the doorway. His phaser hung loosely in his hand.

Spock climbed back up on the lift and recommenced his analysis of the devices inside the computer node. There was one cluster consisting entirely of omnidirectional diodes. Several of the components formed advanced forcefield projection units and graviton beam emitters. There was also a targeting scanner, with a protected feed through the rock ceiling.

As absorbing as his investigation was, Spock was distracted by the captain's pacing through the chamber. After a while, as Kirk continued his restless back-and-forth march, Spock finally leaned over the railing of the lift. "You are disturbed, Captain. May I be of assistance?"

"Find me that computer, Spock. I want to see the machine that's capable of transporting a starship a thousand light-years away."

Spock knew there was no need to correct Kirk's approximation at this moment. "I am currently endeavoring to do so, Captain."

"Yes, I know, Spock. But it makes me antsy to be sitting on top of that much power. It's here—somewhere—and we have to find it." Kirk narrowed his eyes. "That energy burst was off the scale. Somebody's bound to come looking for what caused it."

"Indeed, that is a reasonable assumption, Captain."

Kirk glanced over at the stash of phasers the *Enterprise* had sent down, then at Reinhart, who was watching the doorway. "Our position is too vulnerable." He flipped open his communicator. "Kirk to *Enterprise*."

"Scotty here, Captain."

"Any sign of ships in this sector?"

"No, sir!"

Spock discerned relief in the engineer's voice. Apparently Kirk heard it, too. "We're lighting up the sensors down here, aren't we?"

"Aye, Captain, yer lifesigns read clear though the rock. The tricorders and diagnostic unit are also sending out power spikes."

Kirk considered the options. "Scotty, tell me more about that portable shield you've been working on."

Scotty's voice warmed like he was talking about an old friend. *"She's making progress, Captain! I just finished synchronizing th' forcefield frequencies to conceal the phase rotation."*

"The question is, Scotty, does it *work?* Can it hide the entrance to this station?"

"She's got a few bugs yet, sir. But I think she'll do the trick for ye," Scott said approvingly. *"Ye never know who might come nosing around at this end of th'quadrant. The Klingon border isn't far from here."*

Spock believed it was a measure of Kirk's agitation that he agreed, "Send it on down, Scotty."

Kirk figured it was worth a try. Scotty had pulled off miracles enough times before that he wouldn't doubt his chief engineer now.

Not long after Scotty signed off, a bulky gray unit materialized on the polished floor of the chamber. It was a double square joined together by a fat Y-junction. There were several aerial feeds on top. The dials on the side were activated, and the power cells were fully charged.

Kirk circled it. The unit didn't look very impressive. Was this why Scotty had spent every off-duty day in the engineering lab rather than relaxing and joining crew activities?

"Reinhart, you're with me." Kirk grabbed one handle of the portable shield unit while Reinhart took the other. Spock raised one brow, making a silent commentary on the probable effectiveness of Scotty's latest pet project.

Kirk gave Spock a warning look, and the Vulcan complacently returned to his examination of the computer node in the ceiling. Now that the neat cubical covering had been removed, the node looked like an explosion of monofilaments and inverter nodules.

Reinhart helped Kirk carry the shield unit up the passageway that doubled back to the doorway. Kirk realized something was different—it was darker in the passageway than before.

It turned out that the door was down, shutting them inside the station. But as Kirk and Reinhart approached, the panel abruptly slid up into the rock. After a moment, the large slab that concealed the doorway moved aside.

"It must be automated," Reinhart ventured.

The dusty surface of the planetoid was the same. The sky was in its "night" phase, which was only slightly darker than normal. The yellow-blue blades of grass growing in the lower cracks of the rocks appeared to be barely clinging to life.

Reinhart looked around with interest, having never seen the surface of the planetoid before. "Where do you want this, sir?"

"Over here." Kirk was trying to remember the instructions Scotty had poured through the communicator. In his opinion, Scotty needed to scale down on the operating requirements to make the shield more user-friendly.

He and Reinhart carried the shield unit to a spot just outside the sliding rock slab. It would probably close again once they went inside, and would add another layer of protection for the landing party.

Kirk activated the levelers and checked the imager to make sure the shield would encompass the entire rock mass. There was room to spare, so he tightened the parameters. Reinhart took care to stand inside the area Kirk indicated. Then it took numerous tiny adjustments to get the gauges pointing in the same direction.

Finally Kirk opened his communicator. "Scotty, we're going under the shield. Maintain an open channel at all times."

Kirk activated the shield. A hum rose from the unit, and a faint pearlized sheen appeared. From the outside, everything would look exactly the same, with the shield unit concealed within. Or so Scotty said. Kirk sniffed. It smelled like hair was burning, but he could see no smoke coming from the unit.

"What do you get, Scotty?" Kirk asked.

"Sensors reading no life-forms, Captain. No power spikes. She did it!" His voice broke with emotion. *"That's a fine piece of machinery, sir!"*

It didn't take much to make Scotty happy. Just a few circuits and microchips did the job. "Good work. Kirk out." He was pocketing his communicator. "Well, that will—"

The doorway slid down and the rock slab suddenly began to move. Kirk pushed Reinhart out of the way. They both ended up tight against the shield, with the rock slab passing inches in front of their noses. It stopped short of the shield unit.

"Sir?" Reinhart asked uncertainly.

Kirk hadn't expected the rock slab to close until they were inside, but he wasn't going to admit that to his security guard. The shield would let them step through, from the inside out. But then they wouldn't be able to get back in again until someone inside the station deactivated the shield.

"We got in before, Reinhart, we'll get in again."

"Yes, sir . . . but how?" Reinhart was splayed against the rock slab.

Kirk was similarly stuck. Whenever he brushed against the shield, there was static discharge.

He tried to remember what had happened when the landing party had found the entrance to the Kalandan station. "We were tracking the power surge, and the indicator on my tricorder pointed directly to this rock outcropping."

"Do you have your tricorder?" Reinhart asked hopefully.

"It's inside."

"Oh." Reinhart shifted, sending up a few static sparks. He pressed his lips together against an unseemly exclamation.

"It was the only time the power surge didn't disappear, so we were able to track it." Kirk thought hard about what he'd done. "We walked right up this slab. The tricorder said the entrance was here—"

The rock slab shifted. Kirk peeled himself off the shield, pulling Reinhart with him. Then the doorway slid up, revealing the passageway into the station.

Kirk straightened his uniform. "An effective system, I'm sure Mr. Spock would say."

"Yes, sir," Reinhart said, in obvious relief.

As they reentered the main chamber, Spock glanced down. "Any trouble, Captain?"

"None, Mr. Spock."

Reinhart took a deep breath. Whatever he had been about to say was lost in his shout. "Watch out! She's back!"

The humming came from the wall behind Kirk, where Losira appeared. He saw right away that it wasn't the deadly replica, but merely an image on the wall. Losira's beauty always had the same impact. There was something very appealing about the way her eyes slanted upward at the outer edges. He even liked the streaks of pink and green, and that unusual purple uniform.

Reinhart had his phaser out, pointing it at the rock wall. Spock also turned, aiming his tricorder at the image.

Her lips opened briefly in a slight smile. *"My fellow Kalandans, welcome. A disease has destroyed us. Beware of it. After your long journey, I'm sorry to give you only a recorded welcome . . ."*

"It's the same message," Kirk said. "It must have been triggered by our entrance."

Spock agreed. "Which means this image is controlled by other means than this damaged computer node."

"Perhaps the computer is capable of repairing itself."

That wasn't exactly a comforting notion, considering how the computer had operated.

"Unlikely," Spoke replied. "I am not reading any energy emissions from this computer node. It is currently inert."

The image of Losira was saying, *"The computer will selectively defend against all life-forms except our own. My fellow Kalandans, I, Losira, wish you well."* Losira closed her eyes and stood impassively, waiting as she had for hundreds of years.

"Did your tricorder get all that, Mr. Spock?" Spock nodded affirmatively. "Send it to the *Enterprise.* I'll include it in my subspace report to Starfleet. They must be informed that a weapon of this power exists."

After a few moments, Losira's image disappeared. Kirk figured that would be the last time he ever saw her. But if they could penetrate this station somehow, there might be more wonders to discover.

Kirk settled onto a folding stool near the lift unit while Security Guard Reinhart resumed his post, keeping watch on the entrance. With a minimum of words, Kirk recorded his message to Starfleet and filed his log on the communications unit. He added the log Spock had kept while he was in command of the *Enterprise.* As auxiliary documents, Kirk included Losira's message and Dr. McCoy's specs on the deadly organism.

Kirk concluded his message by saying, "I believe this station is worth further investigation, if only to ensure that the defense system is fully deactivated. Request permission to remain in this sector. Another ship can take over our diplomatic assignment in the Cister system." They would be late reporting to that engagement now, at any rate. "I await your decision. Kirk out."

Kirk sent the message to Uhura on the *Enterprise,* asking her to encode it at the top security level. No need to let anyone else know about the incredible technology concealed on this planetoid.

Kirk was dozing fitfully when Spock informed him that the *Enterprise* had signaled with a coded transmission that had arrived from Starfleet Command. Kirk stumbled up from the bedroll, noting that both Sulu and McCoy continued to sleep. Even Reinhart was snoring lightly, slumped in his post near the entrance. Only Spock continued to work.

Kirk sat down with the portable communications unit to listen to the message. It was from Commodore Enwright, which meant Starfleet considered this to be a matter of galactic defense. Enwright's smooth, dark face was impassive as usual, giving no indication of his inner thoughts. But Kirk could guess at the commodore's mood; Enwright was known for his sour temper and rigid adherence to duty.

"Captain Kirk, send a full report, including technical data regarding the interstellar transporter you have discovered. Do not, I repeat, do not allow that technology to fall into enemy hands, especially those of the Klingons or the Romulans. We must protect the balance of power in this quadrant. Understood?" the commodore demanded.

Kirk understood. The Romulans could use an interstellar transporter to send assassins into the very heart of the Federation. The Klingons would undoubtedly want to know the secret of cellular disruption, to incorporate it into their own weapons.

Armed with his orders, Kirk went to help Spock assemble the technical data they had acquired thus far. It was up to him to make sure the Kalandan station was protected.

Chapter Two

TASM OF THE Petraw scout ship *Y8847* was on duty at the subspace post, monitoring sensors and communications. She methodically traced each of the hundreds of subspace messages their ship intercepted, rejecting each one when it originated in a location outside the targeted sector.

Then the computer flashed an alert. Finally, a subspace message from the targeted sector had been located. It was what the Petraw had been waiting for.

It wasn't long ago that her pod-mate Kad had been on duty at the subspace post when sensors detected a power surge of immense strength. The magnetic burst had been too brief to give them much information, but Kad had traced it to its source in a sector seven light-years away. Luz, who was at the helm, had turned their scout ship toward that system, and they were proceeding there at full speed. Since most of their scout ship was devoted to engines, they could easily move three thousand times the speed of light. They had already left behind the territory documented by other Petraw scouts.

Tasm tracked the progress of the encoded message through their ship's decryption nodule. It was a classified communiqué from something called the Federation *Starship Enterprise* to Starfleet Command. Its origin appeared to be from precisely the same coordinates where the computer had pinpointed the source of the power surge.

It was absolutely silent in the small control booth, yet Tasm could tell that the others knew she had detected something. Her other pod-mates Pir and Marl, seated at the engineering post and navigational control, looked no different. Their expressions were rather blank, as usual. But she could tell by their tense shoulders and sidelong glances that they were eager for a new mission.

Tasm felt herself flush yellow, and she stood straighter at her post. Yet she did not intend to inform them that she had intercepted a subspace message until her analysis was completed. She was taking control of this engagement, as per their training. She and her pod-mates could assume any post, as they were equally adept at every ship's function. The first member of the pod to make contact with an alien species or locate an opportunity for acquiring new technology became their leader.

Tasm had been the leader on a few engagements before. The last one had been when their ship encountered an Andorian merchant deep in the Beta Quadrant. After only one subspace discussion, Tasm knew that the way to get technological information from the Andorian was to let him take advantage of them in a trade. Their ruse had worked, and on completion of the engagement, they had acquired the Andorian's unusual ship. They had sent it back to their Petraw birthing world via automated drone. The Andorian had been stranded on a Class-M planet, and would undoubtedly survive, living among the native animal-plants. If he didn't die from lack of companionship. Tasm had never met an alien who liked to talk more than that Andorian. She rarely thought about him now.

Tasm downloaded the information gathered by previous Petraw scouts concerning "Starfleet Command." There were two recorded Petraw engagements with Starfleet, and both had succeeded in a minor way. The Petraw had managed to conceal their identity, but had gained only a few technological devices.

Apparently Starfleet was the quasi-military arm of the United Federation of Planets. They weren't particularly acquisitive, though they were curious. The other two Petraw leaders had found it difficult to acquire technology from the Starfleet officers they had encountered.

Key to understanding Starfleet was something called the "Prime Directive." They were very possessive about their technology, excusing their unusual behavior by insisting it could interfere in the cultural or technological development of an alien species. But Starfleet could also be generous to a fault when assisting people in a crisis. It was an interesting combination, with plenty of characteristics that Tasm considered exploitable.

Tasm filed the information away for eventual dissemination to the two pods. Meanwhile, the decryption nodule accessed the specs of the Federation's universal translator to assist in unraveling the code.

The decryption nodule performed flawlessly, as

usual. Every Petraw scout was instructed to give priority to acquiring decryption technology. Knowledge was the basis of any successful engagement.

With the message decoded, the Starfleet symbol appeared on the clear polished surface of Tasm's panel. It was followed by a verbal report from a Captain James T. Kirk of the *Starship Enterprise*. He was an ordinary bipedal life-form without any immediately noticeable physical characteristics. The computer indicated he was "human."

The human was seated in a cavernous space very different from the lowering bulkheads the Petraw lived under. It looked like a starship, but on closer inspection, Tasm saw that the upper walls were made of rock. Yet her first impression was confirmed when he began to speak.

> *"Captain's Log, Stardate 5726.4. While transporting down to an unexplored Class-M planetoid to investigate some puzzling geological conditions, there was an unexplained power surge that flung the* Enterprise *nearly a thousand light-years away. The planetoid was manufactured as an advance force station by Kalandan scientists approximately ten thousand years ago. Though the Kalandans died, their automated computer attacked my crew."*

The humanoid went on to summarize the recent events, including their encounter with a remarkable interactive replica. After considering the list of astonishing feats accomplished by the automated computer, Tasm still had her doubts.

She studied the human intently. Comparisons with other humans encountered by the Petraw revealed he was a mature member of that species. He had a decisive manner, and appeared determined to investigate the station even while he and his team were trapped there by a "deadly organism." It was obviously a situation fraught with opportunities for the Petraw. Tasm wasn't counting on anything—often aliens grossly exaggerated the capability of their technological devices. Yet it looked promising, nonetheless.

Tasm was not proud, exactly, to be the leader on this engagement. But she was satisfied to be able to fulfill her natural duty.

Included in Captain Kirk's communiqué was a recorded message that he claimed was made by the Kalandan commander. It was a female humanoid, subtly different from the male human she had just seen. *"My fellow Kalandans, welcome. A disease has destroyed us. Beware of it . . ."*

The computer ran through a comparison to identify previous Petraw engagements with this species. The search was negative. Since the Kalandans had reportedly been dead for ten thousand years, Tasm was not surprised.

The Kalandan female finished her dire welcome speech, then faded from view. There was an assortment of other reports, one made by a crew member called First Officer Spock. This bipedal life-form was different from Captain Kirk. Again, Tasm's search of the Petraw database was negative. So here was another new species for them to deal with. . . .

Her pod-mate Pir made a slight sound, though his bland, yellowish face was expressionless. He was eager to get a new engagement. Who wasn't? They lived for their engagements. Tasm knew her pod-mates as well as she knew herself. She knew their minor weaknesses, like Kad's tendency to fall into meditation while working. Or the way Luz stared at the stars through the port on the docking hatch.

Periodically, when the other pod took over duty in the command booth and ship's maintenance, she and her five pod-mates retired to their cells to meditate on the information feed relayed from their birthing world. Each cell was a deep hexagonal space, with six cells stacked three wide and two high. The other pod of six Petraw who also manned their ship used the same cells. Tasm could touch the ceiling of the cell while lying on her back, with her head cupped by the information feed at the end.

Their cells were exactly the same as the cells on their birthing world. Except back home, the cells were stacked hundreds long and high, filling the chasm adjacent to the underground tunnels. Tasm's pod had worked hard as a unit soon after crawling out of their first cell. As they grew, they cleaned out cells' afterbirths and helped maintain the vast system of life-support tubes that carried food to the young and adult Petraw. After duty shift, they had retired to their cells to be trained as scouts through the information feed.

When their pod was fully grown, they had duties in the training center and experimental stations, where they studied alien works of engineering. They had been involved in repairing, improving, and adapting acquired technology to the needs of the Petraw. Then they were assigned to build scout ships, and eventually they had built their own, with the help of their sister pod.

The twelve Petraw had launched their ship and left the tubes of their birthing world forever. As they ventured further and further away, they sent back technology, specs, and data to their birthing world via automated drones produced by their industrial replicator. It was their life's work.

Despite Pir's impatience, Tasm refused to be rushed. Still standing at her post, she went into meditation to determine their best course of action. She trusted her training, which had equipped her to excel at any duty post on their ship, including that of leader.

A dozen crons later, when Tasm opened her eyes, she had the answer. It was obvious what course of action they must take. They would pose as Kalandans, descendants of the scientists who had created the station. They would claim the remarkable technology on the station as their birthright. That would neatly circumvent Starfleet's Prime Directive. And by posing as Kalandans, they would give Captain Kirk what he so clearly wanted—contact with this long-dead species.

Tasm set the parameters of their mission and issued her orders through the information feed to each Petraw. Included in the information feed were the captain's communiqué that he had sent to Starfleet and the message recorded by the female Kalandan. Tasm would determine their individual targets later. However, she intended to personally target their leader—Captain Kirk.

Pir was making small sounds of pleasure as he absorbed the information feed directly from his panel. The other pod-mates were in their cells, meditating on the feed.

Yes, it would be good to have an engagement again. Too many mega-crons had passed since their last one.

Tasm called Kad from the engineering monitors to take over the subspace post, while she went to complete the programming on the surgical unit. This engagement would require a slight alteration in their appearance for them to pose as Kalandans.

The medical alcove finished processing her final physical specifications for the Kalandan species. Tasm stepped into the half-circle niche off the main corridor. Their control booth, meditation cells, labs, access tubes, and replicator stations took only one-tenth of the entire ship. The engines and propulsion unit occupied the remainder.

Several of her pod-mates were waiting in the corridor, having absorbed the information feed in their cells. They were ready for the transformation. Like Pir, some were making slight noises indicating their pleased anticipation of the engagement.

Tasm closed her eyes as she sank her head into the support depression. The surgical unit emitted a glaring array of crisscrossing red lasers that reconfigured her face and hands. Her hands would retain four digits—it was seldom they altered this feature—but the bulbous ends were trimmed to a gentle point like Losira's.

When the unit signaled that the transformation was complete, Tasm stepped out and took in the delight of her pod-mates. She examined herself in the mirrored surface that lowered after her pod-mate entered the surgical unit.

Her face had been changed by a strong chin and jawline. She also had rounded cheeks. Most dramatic were her eyes and brows, swooping up expressively at the ends. The colored swaths on her eyelids were brilliant peach and yellow, complementing her golden skin tone. Great amounts of hair had been attached to her head, and were now swept back in Kalandan-style rolls before falling down her back.

When her pod-mate emerged from the surgical unit, he was a male Kalandan, with the same high cheekbones and slanting eyes. His hair was a shorter version of Losira's, with the bulk rolled back away from his face and tied in a curling tail.

They were both rather blurred copies of the Kalandans, it was true, but they could explain that by the intervening generations since their people had lost contact with the science station.

In high spirits, Tasm led her altered pod-mates down the corridor to the replicator that would create their uniforms. Their usual nudity on board would cease, and they would even meditate in their cells in the required clothing until their engagement was completed.

The replicator modified the Kalandan uniform to their rather spare bodies. It was dark purple and showed no skin, though it had the same wide-legged pants trimmed with silver braid. The uniform also had built-in padding to imitate the Kalandan's exaggerated humanoid sex characteristics. Tasm was amused. The Petraw bodies were sleek in comparison.

Tasm examined the result in the mirror and was satisfied. She knew that sexual attraction could be one key to targeting Captain Kirk. From the specs the computer had given her on humans, his increased pulse and the widening of his pupils when he spoke about Losira indicated his attraction to her. Tasm knew that sexual allure did not depend on physical appearance alone. She could create any impression she wanted to simply by being who Kirk wanted her to be.

Smiling slightly, already sinking into her imitation of the serene and intelligent Losira, Tasm headed back to the control booth to relieve her pod-mates so they could make the transformation and prepare for their engagement.

Chapter Three

SHORTLY AFTER LYING DOWN in the underground station, Sulu woke with a start when Losira began to speak. Her melodious voice caused a surge of panic, as he thought he was going to be attacked. But the captain and Mr. Spock appeared unconcerned. That was when Sulu realized it was the message they had already seen, the one the commander had left to welcome her long-dead compatriots.

Sulu lay back down. Dr. McCoy never stirred, sleeping more soundly than anyone in their position had a right to. Sulu dozed fitfully. The problem of Losira bothered him. How could the Kalandans be so compassionate and yet so ruthless? What kind of people could be technically superior in every way and yet fall prey to total annihilation?

Sulu also couldn't imagine why such an advanced civilization would create a terrible weapon like cellular disruption. It didn't just kill, it caused agony. Even now, after multiple medical regenerations with the ana-

41

bolic protoplaser, his shoulder still sent shooting pains straight into his spine. Sometimes it was so bad he could hardly see. He shuddered at the amount of pain D'Amato, Wyatt, and Watkins must have suffered as they died. Pure torture . . .

After everything that had happened, Sulu wouldn't be surprised to see one of those thick black lines appear, heralding the arrival of the Losira replica. One touch was all it would take to turn him into a dead man.

So Sulu was hardly refreshed when he finally got up from the sleeping mat. The others didn't look like they were thinking much about the danger that lurked in thin air. Then again, he was the only one who knew what Losira's touch felt like.

Dr. McCoy was yawning as he quietly consulted with the medical staff on board the *Enterprise*. The doctors would surely find a cure for whatever had infected them . . . yet Sulu couldn't help but be worried. Losira's people were scientists so advanced that they could fling the *Enterprise* a thousand light-years away. Yet they hadn't been able to fight this deadly organism. How could the medical staff of the *Enterprise* hope to do better?

Sulu wasn't about to voice his misgivings, not when the captain was looking so grim. Kirk had taken his tricorder and was examining the walls, a thoughtful frown on his face. Mr. Spock was still working on the lift, scanning the computer node. The Vulcan had apparently toiled the night through and would continue to keep up that pace until they were able to beam back to the *Enterprise*. Sulu had seen Spock in crisis situations before, and envied his stamina.

The *Enterprise* . . . Sulu hoped it wouldn't be long

before they returned. His breakfast rations sat like a lump in his stomach. He cleared his throat. "Have you found anything, Captain? I wasn't able to detect any variation in the surface."

"Nothing, down to the atomic level." Kirk's eyes didn't leave the tricorder.

Sulu joined him near the back wall. "There must be more to this station than this one room."

"Indeed, Mr. Sulu. The question is where."

Sulu shook his head briefly. "Maybe this isn't the entrance to the station. We could try looking around outside for another door. Those bigger rocks could be hiding other underground chambers."

Kirk smiled briefly. "I suppose we could go around saying 'open sesame' to every rock outcropping. . . ." He suddenly looked up, as if taken with the idea. "Or no . . . what if we tried that in here? The door to this chamber opened when I said, 'The entrance is here.' Perhaps the same command will work inside."

Sulu was doubtful, but it wasn't his place to shoot down the captain's suggestions. "It's worth a try, sir."

"You take that side. I'll start over here," Kirk ordered.

Sulu went to the wall where Losira's message had appeared. He felt silly facing the wall, but he heard Captain Kirk's quiet command from the other side of the room. "The entrance is *here.*"

Sulu glanced over his shoulder, but nothing happened. Kirk stepped sideways and continued to face the wall, repeating his statement.

Taking a deep breath, Sulu looked at the pale, shimmering surface and said, "The entrance is here."

Nothing happened.

Now feeling even sillier, he moved aside and tried it again. And again. Security Guard Reinhart quickly finished his morning rations and joined them. He started on the wall next to the passageway.

Sulu stepped past a support beam and continued methodically reciting the words. He wondered how long they would have to do this before they could give up. Kirk was nearly through his second section of wall, while Sulu was moving toward the middle of another section.

"The entrance is here," Sulu doggedly repeated.

A section of the wall abruptly slid up, revealing a door with a rounded top.

Sulu leaped away, tripping over his own feet. He drew his phaser so fast it felt like it materialized in his hand. "Captain! I've found something."

Captain Kirk was already striding over. "So I gathered, Lieutenant." His phaser was also in his hand.

They stared into the darkened space, but there was nothing to be seen beyond a few meters where light slanted in from the entrance chamber.

Kirk gestured with his phaser. "Sulu and Reinhart, you're with me."

Sulu glanced back at Mr. Spock, but he was already returning to his work. The Vulcan was curious, but he was even more self-disciplined. But Sulu wasn't surprised when McCoy strained to see after them. The doctor liked to be involved in everything the captain did.

As soon as Kirk stepped over the threshold, recessed lights came on. They ran in a strip down the center of the corridor. The walls were straight, curving overhead to meet the ceiling. Sulu aimed his tricorder at the closest surface and found it was made of plasticized osmium. An unusual choice of building materials. But that's what gave the walls their milky white surface. Beneath that was the usual diburnium-osmium alloy.

The corridor slanted downhill. Sulu didn't notice it at first, but after a few steps, he could feel it in his legs. The ceiling seemed to press down overhead. When he looked back, the doorway was slightly above him.

The walls were marked every so often by black lines, delineating doors opening off the corridor. Kirk went to the first door and it slid up automatically. Cautiously, holding his phaser ready, the captain stepped inside.

The tricorder was reading no energy emissions. Sulu followed, curiously looking around the long, wide chamber. It had waist-high counters against the walls, with panels above and below indicating storage. Kirk opened the closest one, and an entire atomic microscope slid forward and settled down on the counter.

Sulu smiled. "Here's one of those science labs we've been looking for."

"Everything a scientist needs." Kirk touched the next panel, which opened to reveal a spherical unit that looked like a laser gene-slicer. The next panel held a photosynthesis meter.

Sulu was opening panels at the other end of the room. "There must be ten fully equipped science stations in this one room."

"It's certainly efficient, as Mr. Spock would say."

They closed the panels and proceeded to check the other rooms that lay behind the doors. Ten rooms in all, with ten stations in each one. The soft lighting was augmented by stronger spots that clicked on whenever equipment was pulled out. The air didn't seem stale, as one would expect from the lack of circulation. Sulu could almost imagine the labs were still in use. It would be a pleasant place to work, with nice, high ceilings and a comfortably padded floor.

Everywhere he looked there was evidence of the long-dead Kalandan scientists. The normal detritus of life had gathered on the shelves and under equipment. The Kalandans favored decorations of once-live vegetation encased in bubbles or pressed flat in plastex cards. There were even a few millennium-old sealed food containers. Sulu carefully avoided touching these, wondering if the atomic structure had degraded enough for them to explode at a touch. He scanned them and found nothing but dust inside.

Despite thorough scans, Sulu could find no genetic material, not even a strand of hair. Quite likely the proteins and organic compounds had degraded over the centuries. That more than anything made it real—the weight of the years since the station had been inhabited had left it sterile. Except for the deadly parasites.

"It *is* a ghost station," he murmured. That's what Kirk had called it on the bridge before they beamed down. Proof once more of the captain's incredible instincts.

Sulu gazed at a spectroscope, knowing that Losira could have stood right here. If she hadn't, some of her fellow scientists had. It made their ruthless computer seem even more puzzling.

They found lots of strange devices they couldn't explain, and Sulu carefully scanned their components for further study. They also found bins of raw material, some with the elements still sealed in condensed stasis blocks, ready to be tapped and used in the Kalandan experiments.

"There's one thing missing," Sulu said after they had finished searching each room.

Captain Kirk was way ahead of him. "There's no access ports to the computer. Or screens for interactive communication. Nothing."

"But they must have had a way to record the results of their experiments," Sulu protested.

Reinhart was holding up a few circular cards that had magnetic crystalline cores. "These sure look like data discs. But where do they go?"

The captain shook his head. "Perhaps they used personal computers. Handheld devices."

Sulu glanced in another cupboard. "Why haven't we found one, left behind on a shelf or something?"

"That's a mystery to be solved, Lieutenant."

They left the science labs and proceeded to the end of the corridor. Here was another flattened, oval chamber, similar to the entrance chamber that housed the computer node. But this one didn't have a node. The ceiling was a smooth arch, just like the corridor.

"Back to where we started." Sulu morosely rubbed his shoulder. It was throbbing in pain from his exertions.

"Not quite, Mr. Sulu. There must be another door in here leading deeper into the station."

Sulu knew that was probably true, but he couldn't help feeling daunted. "Sir, this planetoid is the size of Earth's moon. If we have to search for every door, it's going to take forever to explore this place."

"Think of it as a treasure hunt, Mr. Sulu. This treasure's been buried for ten thousand years, so it's worth some extra effort."

"Aye, sir." Sulu couldn't disappoint the captain.

Kirk slung the tricorder over his shoulder. "I'm going to show Mr. Spock the readings of the science labs. You two continue on," he ordered. "Keep me informed."

"Aye, sir," Sulu acknowledged, along with Reinhart's brisk response.

Kirk disappeared back down the corridor. The doorway stayed open.

Nodding to Reinhart, Sulu strode to the far end of the chamber and faced the wall.

"The entrance is *here*." He said it with much more certainty now. The captain was right. They would find what lay beyond if they just kept trying.

Spock looked up from his diagnostic unit as Captain Kirk returned. Dr. McCoy was far more eager as he left his temporary medical lab to join the captain. "What did you find, Jim?"

"Science labs," Kirk replied. "Some of the best-equipped labs I've ever seen. You should take your gear in there, Bones, and set up."

McCoy headed to the open door and the corridor beyond. Spock appreciated the doctor's absence, and hoped it would be lengthy. McCoy's muttering as he monitored the growing cultures in the bio-trays had become almost annoying.

"We also found these discs, Spock." Kirk splayed a handful of circular cards. "But we couldn't find any computer access ports."

"The communications unit has an interface port," Spock reminded him.

Kirk handed Spock the tricorder he had taken into the labs. "Here, take a look at the equipment we found in there."

Spock examined the readings while the captain fed one of the circular discs into the interface port on the communications unit. It took some adjustments to initiate the interface. "That should do it," Kirk said. "We'll let that—"

The communications unit let out a series of rapid beeps, indicating there was a malfunction. After a moment, a wisp of smoke appeared from the aperture. Hastily, Kirk ejected the circular disc. From the way he tossed it from hand to hand, then dropped it, Spock ascertained that the casing was hot.

Spock picked up the disc. It was currently 132 degrees and cooling rapidly. The plasticized osmium casing had melted and twisted from the heat.

"Intriguing," Spock commented. "The disc must possess an internal energy source, to be capable of self-destructing."

Kirk was looking doubtfully at Spock's fingers as he held the hot disc. "Quite the defensive-minded people, these Kalandans."

"Undoubtedly." Spock examined the tricorder readings of the labs. There were unusual features in each of the devices. "This equipment appears to be designed for botanical studies."

"Botany?" Kirk asked. "On a space station?"

"Apparently the Kalandans were well-rounded in their scientific inquiry." Spock nodded over the list of devices. "Quite thorough, in fact."

"As soon as I saw those labs, I knew you'd appreciate them."

Spock raised one brow in question. "This station has survived without maintenance or sentient guidance for over ten thousand years. Surely that is an accomplishment to be admired."

"Admired, yes," Kirk said shortly. "I wish we could see more of it. Sulu and Reinhart are continuing the search. We found another sort of . . . nexus chamber, like this one. Only it doesn't have a computer node." Kirk nodded toward the detached cube. The colors seemed to move even more sluggishly. "What have you found?"

Spock turned to the white node. "This node is not the source of the Losira images. However, it did target and focus the energy of the computer. I also believe this node targeted the *Enterprise* for interstellar transport."

"How does it work, Spock?"

"In much the same way our tractor-emitters focus on a remote target and use a superimposed subspace/graviton force beam to move an object. This device focused the energy force beams and allow them to be transmitted to the target."

"Like a valve or a gateway," Kirk agreed. "That's why our tricorders read the energy spike like a door opening, then shutting."

"Precisely, Captain." Spock gave the node an admiring glance.

"Can you tell where the energy beam originated from?"

"Negative." He indicated a precise spot in the wall. "The monofilaments go through a stasis junction here, beyond which our sensors cannot penetrate. The reason is currently unknown. However, I may have a solution."

Spock went to workspace built into the side of the lift. There he had placed one container of medical nanites.

"These are nanites," he explained to Kirk. "Submicroscopic robots that are manufactured in Dakar, Senegal, and used for medical functions. Dr. McCoy has been attempting to use them to isolate the virus."

Dr. McCoy returned from the science labs just in time to overhear. "What have you got there, Spock?" As he drew closer, his eyes widened. "Those are my nanites! What are you doing with them?"

"I was assessing their usefulness in penetrating the monofilaments of the computer node." Nanites were not easy to obtain, and Spock held on to the self-programmable container firmly. He wouldn't put it past the doctor to claim ownership, despite his pressing need. "They are small enough to enter the monofilaments. I intend to program them to trace a path to the source of the energy."

McCoy hesitated. "I guess they could be used for that. Here, give it to me." He took the container from Spock and programmed it. "I'm setting their functions for vascular work. The nanites will run through the tubes until they reach a blockage, where they'll attempt to clear it and continue on. They won't be able to do much for damaged monofilaments."

"I am not attempting to repair the system, Doctor. Please activate the subspace beacons so the nanites can be traced."

McCoy glanced up. "Whatever you say, Spock. But you know these things don't go very fast. It could take hours for them to get anywhere."

"Depending on how far away the energy source is from this location, I estimate it will take up to five days, four hours and twenty-two minutes."

"Well!" Kirk exclaimed, smacking his hands together. "It looks like you have this under control, gentlemen. Carry on, Spock. Bones, do you need help moving into one of the science labs?"

"Sure, Jim," McCoy agreed, distracted from Spock's work. Spock didn't pay much attention as the doctor began enthusing to the captain over the Kalandan labs. Kirk picked up the medical diagnostic unit and carried it toward the corridor, while McCoy followed with some trays of his growing samples.

Spock was satisfied, preferring to work with the node alone in this chamber.

Then a call came from the corridor. "Captain! Captain Kirk!"

Sulu appeared in the darkened doorway leading from the entrance to the main chamber. "Captain, come look! I think we found something."

Chapter Four

"WE FOUND A ROOM with a command chair," Sulu told him.

Kirk hoped this was the break they'd been looking for. "Lead on, Mr. Sulu," he ordered. "Mr. Spock, Dr. McCoy, you're with us."

"It's about time!" McCoy exclaimed. Kirk was well aware that the doctor didn't like being stranded from the *Enterprise*. This mission had lasted far longer than any of them had anticipated.

Sulu briskly led the way down the long corridor lined by the open doors to the botany labs. In the oval chamber beyond, an open doorway had appeared in the left-hand side. Kirk noted that the smooth, curved ceiling continued as the door led to another corridor. It was a bit wider than the ones on board the *Enterprise*. It slanted like the first corridor, taking them farther underground.

McCoy had one brow raised. "The Kalandans liked to keep it simple, didn't they?"

As he walked, Spock's eyes were fastened on the screen of his tricorder, analyzing the environment. "Far from simple, Doctor. The complex alloy of diburnium and osmium is impervious to our phasers."

Sulu glanced over his shoulder nervously. "They weren't fooling around when they made this station, were they?"

"No," Kirk agreed grimly. "The Kalandans must have had some pretty ferocious enemies."

"We didn't touch the command chair," Sulu assured him. He shuddered slightly at the thought of what could happen next.

McCoy was blinking faster, obviously rethinking his desire to accompany them.

"Anything else?" Kirk asked Spock.

"My tricorder is reading unusual energy vibrations within the alloy. I am unable to pinpoint the source." Spock seemed more interested in his tricorder than the relentlessly white corridor.

When Kirk touched the wall, the upper plasticized osmium layer didn't even smudge. It was dry, and left no residue on his finger. When he looked back, the hallway curved up out of sight. It was a very long and empty corridor.

"Here it is," Sulu announced as they went through another doorway.

Reinhart was waiting in the chamber. It was about six meters across and perfectly round. In the center of the smooth arch of the ceiling was another computer cube. This cube was pulsing rapidly with colored light.

Reinhart had his phaser out and was aiming it warily at the computer cube. His back was against a wall, and he kept glancing around as if expecting one of the

Losira replicas to suddenly appear. When they arrived instead, Reinhart breathed a sigh of relief. Sulu also seemed to have had his doubts that Reinhart would still be here when he returned.

Kirk was determined not to run scared from a computer replica. He walked directly into the chamber.

Spock followed, aiming his tricorder at the computer node. "This computer node is in a standby phase." The others relaxed somewhat at that.

The only thing in the room was a white molded chair directly underneath the cube. It seemed to be part of the floor, as if the plasticized covering had been draped over a chair while it was soft. The arms gleamed whitely with no sign of buttons or screens.

"Look, Jim!" McCoy pointed at the faint gray circle around the chair. "What do you think that is?"

Spock aimed his tricorder down. "There is a magnetic-powered mechanism concealed beneath the chair."

Kirk traced his finger on the line. "What does it do?"

"Unknown, Captain," Spock replied.

The ominous never-ending pulsing of the computer cube accompanied his approach to the front of the chair.

"You're not going to sit down!" McCoy protested. "What if it drops you into a black hole or something?"

"Do you have a better idea, Doctor?" Kirk waited, but no one offered anything. "Mr. Spock, once that computer is activated, get whatever readings you can from it. Reinhart, fire at the computer node only on my order."

"Aye, sir!" Reinhart replied as Spock readied his tricorder. "Ready, Captain."

Kirk knew anything could happen when he sat down in the chair. But that was just one of the benefits of being captain of the *Enterprise*.

Kirk slid into the chair. It was dry, yet slippery; he almost had to hold himself on the seat.

The chair started shaking along with the floor, throwing his men off balance. Kirk braced himself, but the tremor didn't reach the heaving pitch it had the first time, when the *Enterprise* was flung one thousand light-years away. It was more like the minor seismic aftershocks they had experienced while the landing party was trapped on the surface.

For a moment nothing happened. Then a thin horizontal line appeared in front of him. It expanded to reveal the Losira replica.

"Captain! Watch out!" Sulu shouted, pulling his phaser from his belt.

Reinhart raised his own phaser, shifting it from Losira to focus on the cube over Kirk's head.

"Don't shoot!" Kirk ordered. Spock's tricorder was whirring as the shimmering cube leaped and danced with colors. There appeared to be an increase in the flashing lights overhead, but Kirk was not about to look away from the Losira replica.

There was a breathless moment as everyone waited for those deadly words from her lovely mouth—"I am for you, James T. Kirk!"

But she said nothing. She merely stood there, expectant and waiting.

"Spock, are you reading anything?" Kirk asked.

"The computer appears to have engaged an interactive node, Captain. I am unable to access a database."

Kirk kept watching Losira. Her purple uniform was

the same, with the short bodice that revealed her midriff above the wide-legged pants. Her dreamy smile was also the same, yet now there was a difference in her demeanor. Her sadness was gone. She seemed relaxed, almost happy, waiting for him to speak. Her hands were lightly clasped together in front of her instead of shaking as they strained to try to touch him.

"Losira?" Kirk asked cautiously.

"Yes, I am Commander Losira's replica." She was perfectly poised, no longer tormented inwardly, as the other replicas had been. "I am here to assist you."

"Assist us?" McCoy muttered. "Then how about giving us a way to get rid of this deadly organism?"

Spock commented, "Doctor, if the Kalandans had possessed the antidote, they would have undoubtedly used it themselves."

Losira appeared not to have heard the exchange. Her eyes were fixed on Kirk's. So he asked, "What do you know about the deadly organism that's on board this station?"

Now Losira's expression became downcast. "Our scientists have been unable to find a way to eliminate the deadly organism from our bodies."

"Where did it come from?"

"We believe it was inadvertently bio-engineered during the terraforming of the planetary surface. As part of our scientific research, our advance force gathers plant samples from the worlds we visit. Some of these new samples are bio-engineered, and the organism most likely emerged from one of these experiments."

Losira turned and gestured.

One section of the wall disappeared, making Sulu gasp out loud. It felt as if they were standing on top of a towering gray rock, looking over the surface of the planetoid. Kirk recognized the purplish sky and the looming rocks, but the flora was astonishingly different. Blues and yellows dominated, with a diverse array of climbing vines and flowers. The golden grasses were taller than their heads, topped by a feathery plume of neon-blue seeds. Most impressive were the slender tree-ferns that towered above the rocks.

"Is that what the surface used to look like?" McCoy blurted out.

The Losira replica didn't answer, so Kirk said, "It's changed a bit."

"This image was ordered taken on cycle 18903," Losira confirmed. "It is currently cycle 22567."

Spock noted the dates down with interest. "Fascinating."

"How did you create an atmosphere for this planet?" Kirk asked.

"The atmosphere and ambient light is maintained by the magnetic field of this planetoid."

"But there is no magnetic field around this planet," Kirk protested. That was one of the peculiarities that had prompted the landing party investigation.

Losira smiled. "The magnetic field is inverted and channeled within the planetoid to power the station."

Spock was nodding thoughtfully. "Captain, that would explain the magnetic sweep in power readings whenever the computer is activated."

Kirk leaned forward. This replica was a font of knowledge. "Where are the engines that convert the magnetic power into energy?"

"That information is controlled by the defense computer," Losira smilingly demurred.

"Well, let me talk to this defense computer."

Losira gazed past him, as if thinking hard about something. As she blinked, the pink and green stripes on her eyelids seemed to flash. After a few moments, she replied, "The defense computer is currently malfunctioning."

Kirk glanced at Spock. "Perhaps when we damaged the computer node, that affected the defense computer."

"It is possible, Captain."

"Good!" Dr. McCoy said emphatically. Sulu and Reinhart shifted uneasily, probably in agreement with McCoy.

"There must be some way . . ." Kirk asked Losira. "Tell me more about your interstellar transporter. How can you transport an entire starship one thousand light-years away?"

Spock murmured, "Nine-hundred-and-ninety point seven light-years, to be exact, Captain."

Losira replied again with a slight smile. "That information is controlled by the defense computer."

"How about a map of the station?" McCoy suggested. "Then we could find the transporter ourselves."

Kirk impatiently repeated McCoy's request for a map of the station.

"That information is controlled—" Losira started to answer.

"Don't tell me," Kirk interrupted. "By the defense computer. So what *can* you tell me?"

"I maintain the command center for this station," Losira replied.

Spock commented, "An evasive response, Captain."

"Yes, I see," Kirk agreed. "What functions take place in this chamber?"

Losira's smile deepened, as if glad that he had finally hit on something she could answer. "A variety of functions can be commanded from this point."

Kirk suddenly felt his chair move. He gripped the armrests, noticing that the landing party instantly took defensive postures. Reinhart's phaser swung wildly upward toward the computer cube.

Kirk held one hand out to warn him to desist. Reinhart maintained his alert status.

The chair finished swiveling smoothly, facing Kirk toward a startled Sulu and Dr. McCoy. Behind them, a pie-shaped segment of the wall seemed to melt into a wide screen with a flow of symbols streaming across. It was perhaps two meters wide, while the wall remained smooth and white on either side. Below the screen appeared a narrow counter containing a grid and more symbols.

Spock went closer while Sulu and McCoy warily backed off. His tricorder moved toward the screen until the front end seemed to slide through. It appeared unaffected by the contact. "A hologram, Captain. Much like the Losira replica."

"But the replicas were solid." Kirk remembered how soft Losira's arms had felt when he had touched the replica sent to kill Sulu.

"This one is not." As if to prove it, Mr. Spock walked toward Losira. She acted as if she couldn't see Spock while he stepped right through her.

"Perhaps the other replicas needed to be solid in order to administer the cellular disruption," McCoy suggested.

"No!" Kirk exclaimed. "There's something different about this replica. Bones, look at her hand."

McCoy stepped forward. "I don't see anything."

"Exactly. But the other replicas wore a ring."

"Yes . . ." McCoy agreed. "It was a bulky, square thing."

"With a knob on top!" Sulu added. "It was on the hand that touched me."

Kirk nodded slowly. "It was on her right hand, the one she always reached out. That's why I remembered the ring. But this replica doesn't have one."

"So maybe that ring is the cellular disrupter," McCoy said.

"Perhaps, Bones."

Kirk turned his attention back to the image of the screen and control panel. Obviously they couldn't operate it manually if it couldn't be touched.

"What does this screen do?" he asked Losira.

"This is the station's environmental control," she said, moving closer to the control panel.

"What is the status of the environment?" Kirk requested.

Losira tapped lightly on two of the squares of the grid. "The station is currently on standby status, with environmental controls for the interior and exterior of the station on minimum maintenance power."

McCoy said, "Maybe that explains what happened to the plants that used to be on the surface."

"Environmental control," Kirk repeated. "That's not going to help us much."

Losira's expression became reproachful. Truly she was an interactive hologram. "Environmental control regulates internal gravity, atmospheric maintenance, water, lighting, heat, and waste management."

McCoy snorted outright. "Maybe we can take over the station through waste management."

Kirk ignored the doctor. "What else is controlled from this chamber?"

Losira stepped back as the environmental control section faded to white. The pie-shaped segment next to it began to dissolve. "This is the station's communications, both internal and external. Currently it is holding on minimum maintenance power."

"Can you put communications back on full power?" Kirk asked. It would be useful to have an alternative form of communication with the *Enterprise*.

Losira got that faraway dreamy look again. For a few moments nothing happened, then she shook her head regretfully. "The station is currently in top-level defense mode. Access to full power must be routed through the defense computer."

A sudden shifting among the landing party indicated their frustration. But Kirk knew they were on the right track.

Losira stepped away as the communications control panel slowly melted back into the blank white wall. One by one she showed Kirk the control panels for deflector shields, sensors, navigation, and one called science diagnostics. There was also a panel for "molecular resolution" and another for "instrumented probes." Kirk was referred once again to the defunct defense computer, and could get little information from Losira on their specific functions. None of the panels would allow him to upgrade their status above minimum maintenance mode.

"The Kalandans were quite good at security," Kirk decided.

"Affirmative," Spock agreed. "I have been unable to access any data from this interactive node."

Kirk narrowed his eyes. "So there's no panel for power systems or propulsion."

"Nor for weapons or tactics," Spock added.

"Those functions must be controlled by the defense computer." Kirk considered their options, eyeing the impassive Losira replica. "It appears this is going to take more time than I thought. I'm going to keep asking our friend, Losira, some more questions. Bones, you get back to work on that organism. If I find out anything else, I'll let you know."

McCoy looked more eager than he had for days. "I'll have to rerun the tests. Now that we know the organism started out as a plant hybrid . . . well, that could make all the difference."

"Good," Kirk said. "Reinhart, continue the search for other doorways. We'll be trying to access the defense computer, so stay on guard."

Reinhart nodded sharply and turned to leave as Spock spoke up. "Captain, I would like to investigate the replica's assertions that this station is powered by an inverted magnetic field."

"Go, then." Kirk gave a dismissive wave. Only Sulu stayed in the control chamber with him.

As the other men left, Kirk thoughtfully turned back to Losira. What an intriguing combination—so sensuous and beautiful, yet impenetrable. "Are you up for a round of twenty questions, Mr. Sulu?"

"Twenty questions?" Sulu asked, puzzled.

"An old Earth game," Kirk explained. "We played it when I was a boy. You get twenty questions to try to find out what someone is thinking about."

"Sounds fun," Sulu said doubtfully.

"It's tedious," Kirk replied. "But very useful in some situations."

He rubbed his hands together, ready to start. After all, Losira was just waiting there, like the ancient

Sphinx, concealing the information he needed. If he found the key to unlock those curved lips, then their mission would be completed. "Losira, let's go back to navigation, shall we?"

Obediently, Losira walked over to the proper segment as it shimmered into view.

Kirk grinned. With such an obliging and beguiling creature to work with, how could he fail?

Dr. McCoy hurried back up the long corridor. It seemed steeper going up than it felt coming down. He returned to the stack of medical equipment set up in the first lab next to the entrance chamber. He was glad he finally had a proper work surface.

The first thing he did was call Dr. M'Benga. There were lingering concerns about the Losira replica that had penetrated the *Enterprise;* what if she was a carrier of the deadly organism?

McCoy activated the visual on the communicator unit. It made for easier consultation with his medical staff than an audio-only communicator. He couldn't tell by Dr. M'Benga's expression, but there was good news. *"Dr. McCoy, all decks have been thoroughly scanned and no organism has been detected. No infections have been found among the crew."*

"Well! That's something, at any rate." McCoy knew he sounded more gloomy than he felt. It would have been a disaster for the entire crew to be infected. At least he only had to deal with a limited number of people. Of course, it was his luck that the infected crew members were the top three officers on the ship!

"Let's run some new diagnostics," McCoy ordered. "Take into account that the organism was originally created as part of a botany bio-engineering experiment."

"A plant hybrid?" M'Benga asked in surprise.

"Something like that," McCoy agreed.

"That could certainly change some of our projections." The unflappable doctor actually sounded eager.

"That's what I thought. I'll get you more information soon." *I hope,* McCoy added silently as he signed off.

A plant parasite that appeared to be a virus inside its humanoid host . . . that was a new one for their database. McCoy couldn't find anything remotely similar, but that wasn't a surprise. Every solution they knew about had already been considered and rejected, so, of course, it had to be something new.

McCoy didn't have much more botany knowledge than he'd gained from a few old Academy classes. So he decided to consult with the senior botanist on board the *Enterprise.* Dr. Es was from the Sinoa system.

It wasn't until Dr. Es appeared on the small screen of the communications unit that McCoy remembered Sinoans had eyes that moved in different directions, capable of simultaneously viewing two angles at once. It was a bit disconcerting, because he had trouble keeping track of which eye was looking at him. He also didn't know what to think of Dr. Es's abrupt and critical comments.

"I've officially requested that my team be notified when unknown organisms have been detected," she informed him immediately. *"I've requested it many times. But no one takes botanists seriously."*

"Well, that's all changed now," McCoy assured her. "I'm serious about getting off this planet sometime in the foreseeable future."

"I see. Now that we're suddenly so important, maybe I should requisition more lab space," Dr. Es sniffed.

For some reason—McCoy thought it might possibly be castaway syndrome—there was something arresting about her. She seemed born to take command. Her shock of white hair emphasized her wide-open, roving eyes. She was a very short, slight humanoid, perhaps half his size.

"If you have a space problem, I'll see what I can do," McCoy replied gallantly.

"Sure you will," Es said flatly.

McCoy soon realized that Dr. Es didn't want any reassurance from him and he might as well keep his mouth shut when she made one of her acerbic comments. It was not a pleasant conversation, but the Sinoan was certainly an expert theoretical botanist. And in spite of her prickly manner, she seemed perfectly willing to assist him.

McCoy didn't remember Es speaking so sharply when she had her physical, not long after being transferred to the *Enterprise*. Then she had been polite, just like any other new officer. But interacting with her now, she was so abrasive that he could understand some of those wry comments he had overheard about her in the mess hall.

So McCoy carefully briefed Dr. Es and continued a constant back-and-forth analysis with her as their diagnostic proceeded.

He wasn't sure how long it took. Periodically Reinhart would arrive in the doorway to check on McCoy, once bringing food that he mindlessly ate sitting in front of the communications unit. The security guard continued to look around uneasily, as if expecting a deadly Losira replica to appear any second. McCoy didn't mind how jumpy Reinhart was. Better that than someone who was napping on the job. It allowed him to concentrate solely on his diagnostic of the organism.

"That's it!" Dr. Es finally announced. *"It's a plant virus. Instead of replicating itself locally within the glandular tissue, like normal fauna viruses, it sends out spores. That's why the biofilter detected alien matter even though the virus itself was purged. The spores were still in the host's tissues."*

"But why didn't the biofilter also eliminate the spores?" McCoy demanded.

"They appear to be inert. There are the spores leaving the virus." On the split-screen was an enlarged view of a living virus. Es highlighted a section of the virus wall that appeared to detach from the rest.

On the other half of the screen, one of Es's eyes focused on the readout and the other on McCoy. He tried to ignore her unwavering scrutiny as he concentrated on the image. Suddenly the part that had detached disintegrated.

"It's being broken up," McCoy said. "M'Benga noted that yesterday. We thought it was normal chromosomal shed."

"Some of the spore species break down to microstrands of DNA in order to be transferred to a different location."

"Yes, plasmids they're called, when its virus fragments."

"These fragments are reattached and activated by enzymes emitted by a female spore." Es said it as if it was something everyone should know.

"How are they carried?" McCoy pressed.

"There's lots of different ways. By air, by water—"

"Or blood. This virus infects the host rapidly. It's probably airborne, then it's carried by our blood."

McCoy ran a diagnostic on their blood and got nothing but an alert for alien contamination and those mysterious subatomic anomalies. "Unknown" flashed repeatedly on his diagnostic unit. He had been looking at that word far too much during this mission.

Undeterred, McCoy requested that the *Enterprise* send down a portable fission unit. When it arrived, he slipped the sample into it, intending to split the molecules from each other, then further, into their atomic units. He didn't take his eyes off the fission unit until the readout appeared.

"It's in the gamma globulins!" McCoy exclaimed. "The DNA particles are intertwining with the DNA of the antibodies themselves. The plasmids have a different subatomic vibration." He sent the data directly to Dr. Es's console on the *Enterprise.*

"Confirmed," she agreed. *"That's why the human immune system can't fight it. It would be fighting itself."*

"The biofilter can detect the virus in our glandular tissue and eliminates it. But it can't locate the plasmids until the spore fragments are activated and rejoined."

"It's a good thing the bio-sensors could detect the subatomic anomalies in the plasmids, or you would have transported back onboard the ship," Es commented.

McCoy could imagine. No wonder it didn't matter when the biofilter removed the virus itself. They were walking spore depositories, with the spore fragments uniting to constantly produce new viruses. Those new viruses would migrate to the host's glandular tissue to grow or be expelled on their breath, to infect new hosts.

"How could the Kalandans create something like this?" McCoy asked in despair. "Could it have been some kind of biological warfare?"

Es shrugged and one eye lifted upward, as if she really didn't care to question the erratic nature of humanoid behavior. The other eye was moving as she read the data. *"Hm. This is a real problem, isn't it?"*

"That's an understatement," McCoy agreed. "The virus appears to be incubating now. What will it do?"

"The virus is slow-growing, while reproduction occurs at an accelerated rate." Es continued consulting her own diagnostic. *"The waste plant products are toxic to animal tissues. They build up in the blood, especially interfering with antibody production. The blood is choked, eventually killing the host."*

"If a secondary infection doesn't finish us off first."

"By my estimate, it could take months for the waste to build up enough to kill a humanoid. Once it's in your system, there's no getting it out."

McCoy blinked at the harsh assessment. She had the worst bedside manner he had ever encountered. But that probably didn't matter much when her patients were plants.

The landing party would have to remain isolated, because with every breath they could infect other people. It appeared they were doomed to a long, slow death onboard an alien space station. . . .

"Now what?" Es asked expectantly. She looked like she hadn't had such an exciting afternoon in quite some time.

McCoy thought she'd be wearing a different expression if *she* were the one stuck on the planetoid. "Now I have to give the captain the bad news."

For once, both her eyes focused on him. McCoy was relieved. It felt like she had him outflanked no matter what he did, but suddenly there was sympathy in her voice. *"The crew needs their captain back."*

"Well, I'm not beaten yet," McCoy assured her.

Es nodded. Now that her eyes were still, he noticed they were remarkably dark and tear-drop shaped. Very striking, indeed. *"I'll run some more simulations and see what I can find,"* Es assured him.

Feeling a tiny bit better, McCoy signed off with Dr. Es. But as soon as her image faded, he was faced with the toughest duty he had ever had—giving the captain the bad news. He knew of nothing they could do to get them back to the *Enterprise*.

Chapter Five

THE PETRAW APPROACHED their target, the *Starship Enterprise*. Though the starship continued to defensively scan the sector, they had not yet detected the Petraw. The Petraw scout ship incorporated a parabolic mirror in their deflectors that, along with a course that placed a magnitude-four nebula between them, managed to elude the sensors of the *Enterprise*.

Luz was working in one of the tech-labs when another in a series of intercepted messages was passed through the information feed by Tasm. This message had been sent to the starship from the officers trapped on the Kalandan station. It contained medical data she could feed into the diagnostic unit that was attempting to find a way to nullify the plant virus.

Dutifully, Luz monitored the diagnostic unit while it went through its programmed sequence. Anyone could have done this monotonous work. Mostly she was irritated that she had been assigned to target the human doctor, Leonard McCoy. This message was from him again—an emotional, weary, impatient man. It would be simple to manipulate this target. She wanted a challenge.

The one she was interested in was the Vulcan. It was not every day the Petraw encountered a new species. And his messages were subtle, without the extreme emotional reactions of the humans. But Tasm had ordered Kad to target the Vulcan. That made Kad second-in-command during the engagement.

Tasm had assigned Marl to the officer currently in charge of the starship—Montgomery Scott, Chief Engineer. Marl did have an exceptional gift for diagnostic analysis. Luz might have chosen him over Kad for the chief engineer, if she had been in command. Eager, impatient Pir was assigned to the ship's helmsman, Lt. Sulu, who was currently stranded on the station. That left Mlan, the third female in their pod, without a target. Tasm was holding her in reserve to target any other key individual they encountered during this engagement.

Luz was glad that at least her pod had active command duties. In their last three engagements, her pod had served as support staff while the other pod took the lead. Now, one of the other pod members had been assigned as her assistant. He was practicing human medical terms under his breath while they ran the diagnostic. It was so predictable. He hadn't been assigned his target yet, and he had already picked out his three primary characteristics intended to appeal to a human. One was, unfortunately, a tendency to hum a lilting tune under his breath.

The other two tech-labs were fully staffed, and working on the problem of the plant virus. They would need a neutralizer for the virus in order to be convincing as Kalandans.

That was the first major flaw in Tasm's plan of engagement. What if they couldn't find a neutralizer? They could be stuck lurking behind this nebula for mega-crons!

The others didn't seem to notice there was a problem. They blithely proceeded as if certain that a neutralizer would burst forth from mere good intentions. Meanwhile, Luz smoldered with resentment. She should be in command. At the very least, she should be analyzing the tapes of the Vulcan instead of Kad.

"Why haven't you transformed yet?"

Luz looked up in surprise as Tasm walked into the compact tech-lab. "You said the neutralizer was top priority," Luz protested.

Tasm looked down her nose, a nice effect in her Kalandan guise. Her character was obviously a powerful woman not given to frivolity. "Your priority is to get into character."

Luz didn't reply, acting as if she was busy peering into the diagnostic unit. But her character was being formed. She had analyzed Dr. McCoy with the help of the computer, and had discovered he was fairly typical among humans. To get close to him, she would have to do little more than politely ask about his wants and needs. None of her expertise would be required for this engagement.

While she remained silent, Tasm shifted closer. "Transform into character now."

Luz stood up, restraining any show of annoyance. She didn't look back at Tasm or her assistant as she left the tech-lab. She had done an exceptional job whenever she was leader. Much better than Tasm, that brain-dead automaton. Every one of her pod-mates lacked imagination—she was the only one who bothered to look beyond the walls of their own ship.

Yet Luz didn't protest because that wasn't allowed. Actually, it wasn't even considered by the others. And rather than pursue that unsettling thought, Luz slid into the surgical unit.

It was a tight-fitting space, too close for comfort. Her head was gripped by the support, and she squeezed her eyes shut. The red flashing lasers made her wince. There was no pain, but she could feel the unpleasant sensation of flesh being shifted and molded. She hated the surgical unit.

But it was interesting to see herself in different guises. When it was finally over, Luz examined her Kalandan female face in the reflective surface of the unit. It was a softened version of Tasm's character, with wide-open innocent eyes and a small, full-lipped mouth instead of the usual narrow slit. Her light brown hair was far less dramatic than Tasm's glossy black rolls.

When Luz emerged, naked except for her face, Pir was just going past. His expression moved with exaggerated pleasure. "Looking good!" Then he finished off with a human imitation of a wink.

Luz drew in her breath. "We're supposed to be Kalandans, not humans."

"Our targets are humans," Pir insisted, gesturing to himself. "What do you think? Not bad, huh?"

Luz refused to respond to such weakness. A truly complex character took days of meditation to create and assume.

But Pir wouldn't leave her alone. He followed her down as she walked to the replicator stations to get her uniform. From behind her, he asked, "Did you see the database on Starfleet Academy? Maybe your target went there, too."

"I've accessed the computer," Luz told him. "I have everything I need."

"Let me know if I can help." Pir gave her an encouraging grin.

Luz's faint smile could hardly have satisfied him, but he did finally leave her alone to get her uniform, along with its built-in exaggerated female features.

Her pod-mates were so undistinguished it hurt. Serving with them doomed her career. If only they were smarter, more ambitious, just better somehow—like her, they might have been chosen to serve the matriarchs instead of being sent off as scouts. From that post, she was sure she could have been picked to receive the royal gel and join the birthing chamber. When they were very young and their pod had been assigned to clean the birthing cells, that had been Luz's ambition.

But none of her pod-mates felt the same way she did, longing for something they didn't have. Soon she had stopped talking about her feelings. She knew they watched her all the time, noting how often she deviated from their path. It was frightening. They had lost no member of their pods yet, but Luz knew her pod-mates wouldn't hesitate to put her away if they believed she was defective.

So she had to hold on and not let them know exactly what she thought of them. Luz had lived this way for a long time now, and she could certainly keep it up. Only it got tiresome every now and again to feel how limited her existence really was.

Scotty was not a happy man. The *Enterprise* remained on yellow alert, with warp engines off-line. Many key systems were disabled. It wouldn't have been a problem if he didn't also have to command the *Enterprise*. But with Captain Kirk, Mr. Spock, and Dr. McCoy stuck on the Kalandan station, that's exactly what he had to do.

Scotty had left Lt. Uhura in command of the bridge while he managed repairs to the warp engines and support systems in engineering that had been damaged by Kalandan sabotage. Uhura was keeping watch on the long-range sensors and communications to make sure no one got close to the *Enterprise* while she was disabled.

Scott hadn't seen the Kalandan lady who had killed his crewmates. It was his constant regret that he had arrived too late to help John Watkins. Engineer Watkins had been a fine lad, he would have gone far, if only . . .

There would be a funeral service for Watkins soon. Since Scotty was in command of the ship, as well as Watkin's superior officer, he was expected to say a few words.

Scotty checked the time and muttered under his breath, "At this rate, we'll never get th' job done!"

"Sir?" asked one of his engineers. She was concentrating on lasering off the securing bolts. Scotty was helping her remove the emergency bypass control valve for the matter/antimatter integrator. It had been completely fused. Scotty still couldn't figure out how the replica had done it. Fusing the integrator required power levels that equaled the entire might of their main phaser banks.

He couldn't wait to get a look at the engines on that Kalandan station. What was it that had produced so much power? He was also deeply impressed by the level of focus and control. The matter/antimatter integrator was barely half a meter across, yet the replica had fused it while they were nearly one thousand light-years away from the Kalandan station. His engineers had been working on getting it off since they had returned to the planetoid, with no luck yet.

"Th' service for Watkins starts soon." Scotty stripped off his gloves. "We'll have to finish this after."

"I think if we take off that edge, we'll be able to get it off, sir," she pointed out helpfully.

"Meanwhile th' ship is sitting exposed." Scotty shook his head in frustration.

At the ensign's concerned expression, Scotty patted her arm reassuringly. "Don't worry, lass. We'll have th' warp engines going soon enough. Now let's get to that funeral service."

At the door to the chapel, Scotty was stopped by Dr. M'Benga. "So what's the word on th' virus?" Scotty asked.

Dr. M'Benga grimly shook his head. "Nothing yet. But now we have the medical and botanical labs working together on it."

With a sinking feeling, Scotty noticed M'Benga seemed quietly desperate—an unusual demeanor for the cool, professional doctor. It looked like the man hadn't slept in two days, and there were deep lines in the dark skin around his mouth. But every wiry black hair was in place, and his blue uniform was crisp.

Scotty knew he was disheveled from working on the engines. He ran a blunt hand through his hair, hoping that would settle it enough for civility's sake. Glancing down, he brushed at the black, powdery streaks across the arms and chest of his uniform, left by the laser residue dusting the integrator.

"Sir, this is about the other deceased crew member," M'Benga continued. "Lieutenant D'Amato."

Scotty sighed. "Now what?"

"The transporter chief says the biofilter detects the organism in his tissues. His body can't be beamed onboard."

"But he's been dead for two days, man!" Scotty realized he was talking too loudly when other crew members turned to look at them. From inside the chapel, some of the seated friends and coworkers of Watkins strained to see what was going on.

Dr. M'Benga replied, "The only method we have now of removing the virus is by splitting open the DNA of the gamma globulin molecules. If we did that, D'Amato's body would disintegrate."

Scotty grabbed M'Benga's arm and dragged him a few steps away from the chapel. This time he took the precaution of lowering his voice. "Can't you beam him into stasis or something?"

"I could, on your order, sir." Dr. M'Benga looked unruffled. "However, I must inform you that, in our current state, operating on emergency power, there would be a danger to the crew if the stasis field failed."

Scotty muttered under his breath. "Aye, now that's a pretty pickle, isn't it?"

Dr. M'Benga didn't reply. He merely kept his hands clasped behind his back, waiting for Scotty's order. Scotty almost wished Dr. McCoy were here. McCoy wouldn't hesitate to give a superior officer his opinion.

Scotty perked up. "I know—why not just beam him from th' station directly into space?"

"That would work fine," Dr. M'Benga agreed. "Except that his family wants D'Amato's body returned to Earth for burial."

Scotty was disappointed that his quick fix wasn't going to work. "All right, Doctor, leave him there. None of us are going anywhere until we get th' landing party back."

Dr. M'Benga nodded shortly. "Very well, sir. But you'll have to speak to D'Amato's relatives." Dr. M'Benga narrowed his eyes slightly. "They have asked to know the status of the removal procedure."

Scotty shook his head, raising his hands. "Not me! Interfacing with th' deceased's family, that's yer job, Doctor."

"One I am now relinquishing to you, as commanding officer of this ship." M'Benga sounded fine, but Scotty knew what it meant. Hysterical relatives weren't his forte, either.

"Uh-oh. Well, I canna do it at this moment, can I?" Scotty gestured to the chapel, which was now full and obviously waiting for him.

"I'll send the latest message to your console," M'Benga assured him.

Scotty didn't want to think about it. If this was what Captain Kirk had to deal with, he was more than ready to give the job of command back. Scotty preferred the quiet hum of his engines to dealing with the needs of all these people.

He squared his shoulders, completely forgetting about the black streaks on his uniform, as he marched into the chapel. There were some things a man had to do in life, and saying good-bye to a fellow officer was one of them.

Scotty normally didn't go into the chapel on the *Enterprise* except for funeral services. And he rarely went then, preferring to watch with the rest of the crew on the screens.

Scotty took his position at the front of the chapel. To his left was the panel covering the portal in the hull that the sealed coffin would slide through. The blue seal of the Federation of Planets, along with the Starfleet symbol, were burned into the rounded lid of the silver coffin. Watkins' body could drift for a hundred thousand years and never encounter anyone, the galaxy was that huge. To be alone in space, pilot of your own tiny craft, exploring until the end of time . . . Scotty didn't understand why D'Amato's relatives were denying him that, but to each his own. That's what he always said.

Watkins' friends and crewmates were sitting there, waiting for him to say something profound that would somehow explain this useless death. The yellow alert signal flashed ominously behind him, like a continuous warning that something terrible could go wrong any second.

Scotty took a deep breath. "John B. Watkins died while serving on board th' *Enterprise,* th' best ship in th' fleet. Watkins risked his life like the rest of us, because we believe in what we're doing out here. For that, we honor our shipmate. He was a good engineer and a good lad. He will be missed." Scotty looked around the suddenly silent room, shocked to stillness by his blunt address. "I don' know about you folks, but I'll lift my glass tonight to the memory of John Watkins!"

A rousing murmur of agreement surged through the room. Scotty nodded to everyone and stepped aside to let one of Watkins' friends stand up. She began to sing one of his favorite songs, about longing and lost love.

Scotty knew that Captain Kirk would have made a more fitting statement—the captain surely could talk his way around an idea, making it grand in the telling. But Scotty was pleased that he had said what he felt. He only wished he knew when Kirk, Spock and McCoy would be returning. He would much prefer to make his toast to Watkins while surrounded by friends of his own.

Chapter Six

FOR THE SECOND DAY inside the Kalandan station, Kirk continued to struggle with the Losira replica to try to get more information. Sometime yesterday he had discovered that he could access the commander's logs. After that he had been lost in a whirl of aliens and other worlds as the Losira replica replayed the logs. He learned more about the Kalandan culture and their scientific studies in his late-night session, and he used a tricorder to record each entry for computer analysis.

He was making more progress than Spock, whose attempt to penetrate the computer monofilaments with the nanites had failed. The beacons ceased to broadcast within hours after the nanites had been released, never to be heard from again.

Dr. McCoy and the entire medical and botanical staff of the *Enterprise* weren't having much luck either. The virus was still growing and shedding spores in their systems.

Kirk slouched in the command chair, his chin

propped on one hand. He was almost glaring at the Losira replica as she blithely continued her report on a planet the Kalandans had just explored. It contained silicone-based, rudimentary life-forms, and Losira was remarkably enthusiastic about the dominant species on the planet. They looked like tangled-up worms to Kirk.

The Losira replica held the knowledge he needed to access the rest of the station, but she stubbornly refused to give it to him. Almost every question was now smilingly deferred to the defense computer. Instead he was getting reams of information that wasn't helping him complete his mission. Yet the more he saw, the more he was convinced Starfleet Command needed to know about these people's miraculous feats of engineering.

Kirk did gain some insight. From things Losira said and the number of people she referenced, he estimated that the station had been manned by several hundred Kalandan scientists. Losira also mentioned storage bays on the station, which must be extensive, since the Kalandans had routinely gathered samples of everything they encountered.

It also became clear that the station took up only a tiny fraction of the planetoid. At first, Kirk had believed the planet was hollow, housing the station. But Spock said the planetoid needed significant mass in order to create a magnetic field.

Sprinkled throughout Losira's logs were repeated comments about the shifting magnetic pole of the planetoid, and the current stability rate of the dipolar magnetic field. She gave daily reports on the geomagnetic declination, indicating that this information was key to running the station. Kirk forwarded every reference about the magnetic field to Spock.

"Captain?" Sulu came up beside him.

Kirk grimaced as he straightened up in the chair. "End log," he ordered. The accompanying image disappeared and Losira abruptly ceased speaking, folding her hands in front of her and waiting with a slight dreamy smile.

"Mr. Spock is preparing his preliminary report, Captain."

Spock was attempting to determine if tapping the magnetic flux of a planetoid of this mass could provide the power necessary to fling the *Enterprise* one thousand light-years away.

"What does he think?"

"It appears that his hypothesis is correct. The magnetic field is capable of producing more power than he anticipated."

"So that's something Losira has given us." Kirk narrowed his eyes at the Losira replica. She was perfectly exquisite, and acted as if she could wait forever. But they didn't have forever.

"Reinhart's checked almost the entire length of the corridor, sir. But there's nothing. I don't understand it—even a small station has to have more than a few botany labs!"

"I agree, Mr. Sulu." Kirk tried but couldn't stifle his yawn. "Where did several hundred scientists sleep? Where did they eat? They had to live somewhere."

Losira came alive, her eyes shifting to look at him. "You have been granted access to the living quarters."

"What?" Kirk sat forward, not quite believing his ears.

"You have been granted access to the living quarters," Losira repeated.

At the same time, there was a shout from the corridor. "Captain Kirk! Lieutenant Sulu! Come look at *this!*"

Kirk leaped from the chair, feeling a bit stiff from sitting on the hard surface for hours. Sulu was right behind him.

The sloping corridor had been transformed from a featureless tube into the central spine of a lattice of connecting corridors. As they went forward, they could see doorways lining the side corridors. These corridors went on for a long way, curving out of sight. Periodically they were pierced by secondary corridors running parallel to the main one.

Reinhart rushed down to join them, his eyes wide and phaser in hand. "What happened? Everything just opened up!"

Kirk was grinning. "We finally got what we asked for, Mr. Reinhart. Losira has decided to be helpful, for a change."

The curving walls of the corridors were bland white, just like the main ones. It was starting to be a strain on Kirk's eyes—too much white. Like being trapped in a blinding snowstorm.

But while watching the logs, he had noticed there were moving colors on the walls behind the Losira replica. It looked like the same shifting, glowing colors that ran across the computer node overhead. Perhaps when the Kalandans were alive these corridors had been decorated with similar pulsing patterns.

In that instant, Kirk could imagine what it was like back when the station was full of Kalandans passing each other in the corridors, talking and laughing. Active, vital explorers going about their business, just like his own crew up on the *Enterprise*.

Kirk stepped to the first doorway and went in. The walls were bare and white, molded softly around counters and benches that were lined with thin cushions. He pressed on a cushion, to find it was made of some sort of slippery plasticized material, like everything else on this station.

The room curved in a broad sweep of uninterrupted walls. At the opposite end there was a low platform. It took Kirk a moment to realize it was a bed. There were two packing cartons and a few stacks of cloth resting on the bed. The room had a bare, unlived-in feeling.

"They died." Kirk's throat felt thick. "It happened slowly. They had time to pack up their belongings and prepare for death."

He knew they were thinking of the virus in their own systems. Did the same fate await them?

His communicator beeped. Kirk was glad for the interruption. He flipped open the cover. "Kirk here."

"Scotty here, Captain. Long-range sensors have picked up an incoming vessel. It appears t' be Klingon."

"Klingon," Kirk grimly repeated. Their encounter with the Klingons last month at Beta XII-A had almost ended in disaster. Commander Kang had believed the *Enterprise* had murdered his crew. It wasn't until later that they had realized they were being manipulated by a malevolent energy being that fed off aggressive instincts. Kirk had required the assistance of the Klingon science officer, Mara, in order to call a truce and rid themselves of the hostile entity. If she hadn't been Kang's wife, her influence would not have been enough to sway him.

Kirk was certain that the truce would not hold for

this encounter. Klingons were not disposed to be friendly.

"Is the shield holding?" Kirk asked.

"There's a bit of ion leakage, but it should do, Captain. Unless they walk right up t' it. But we'll have to cease communications. I've already notified sickbay."

Kirk lowered his voice. "We're running out of options, Scotty."

"Understood, Captain. I'll let you know when th' Klingons are gone."

Scotty was nothing if not optimistic. But Kirk slammed his communicator shut. Klingons were approaching and he was stranded away from his ship!

"Now what, Captain?" Sulu asked. Both of them looked worried.

"Now we start searching these rooms," Kirk ordered. "There must be personal computers or recording devices—*something* we can use to access the computer on this station."

"Aye, sir!" Sulu and Reinhart replied at once.

As they left the room, Kirk turned to the containers and began to unload the first one. Anything was better than pacing back and forth in frustration, wondering what was happening to the *Enterprise.*

Captain Mox took the bridge of the Klingon cruiser *'Ong* as they entered the sector where the power surge had been detected. None of his officers met his eyes, including his first officer. Mox remembered Gulda's grin the day he had promoted her, not three duty cycles ago, as they clanged their flagons of bloodwine together.

Now Gulda would not look at him. So went the fleeting pleasures of life. Mox had insisted that his crew follow the code of honor established by Kahless the Unforgettable, even though they weren't believers. Now they were amused that he felt the dishonor of his father's shameful death.

"Report!" Mox roared, glaring at each bridge officer. They shifted and glanced uneasily his way. That was better.

"There is a vessel in orbit around the planet," Gulda announced.

Mox bared his teeth. He had come immediately to the bridge when their sensors had discovered the planet at the source of the power surge. "What vessel?"

"According to the energy signature, it appears to be a *Constitution*-class starship."

"Starfleet . . ." Mox arranged his tattered armor as he sat in the command chair. The others were restless. Starfleet vessels were a match for Klingon battleships, but the *'Ong* was a mere cruiser.

"Stay on course!" Mox ordered. They would regret doubting his leadership. He would not give way to Starfleet. He scorned the Organian agreement that made them keep peace with the Federation, and he spit on Klingons who feared a race that lived halfway across the galaxy. A coerced peace was no peace at all.

The pin-dot planet grew slowly, brightening until it began to take shape as a sphere against the darkness. Odd that it floated free of any solar system. Yet it had an atmosphere like a typical Class-M planet.

"Captain!" the first officer exclaimed, returning to her more familiar tone of voice. "We have confirmation. It's the *Enterprise!*"

The *Enterprise!* Mox felt a rising sense of certainty. This was why he had been called across space. To meet the flagship of Starfleet . . . the most powerful ship in the Federation of Planets.

Mox swung out of his chair and was at Gulda's station in two strides. "Have they seen us?"

"Unknown, Captain." Her fingers flew over the panel, trying to get a tactical reading. "Captain—they appear to be damaged. Warp engines are off-line. They're operating on auxiliary generators."

Mox let his mouth fall open. "It must be a trick . . ."

"No, Captain! They couldn't mask the energy signals from their warp engines. The matter/antimatter reactor is shut down."

Mox felt his chest swell in anticipation. This was it! The flagship of Starfleet was at his mercy. The ghost of his father must surely be at his shoulder, giving him this chance to affirm the words of Kahless and restore honor to his house. It would be a victory that would be hailed by the followers of Kahless across the quadrant!

"The *Enterprise* is hailing us, Captain." Gulda's expression was eager now, as if no shadow of disgrace had ever come between them.

Mox was smirking as he settled into his command chair. "Let's see what the captain of the great flagship has to say."

After some delay, the image of the *Enterprise* faded to be replaced by the head and shoulders of a puny human. His sparse black hair was no adornment for a warrior, and his face was smooth as a baby's. This was the mighty Captain Kirk?

Mox sneered at the human, certain he could prevail over him. "Captain Mox of the cruiser *'Ong.*"

"*Chief Engineer Scott of the* Starship Enterprise."

The man had a strange, lilting accent. *"What's yer business here, Capt'n?"*

A mere engineer. "Where is Kirk?"

The engineer tightened his mouth. *"Well, he's indisposed right now. Ye'll have to make do with me, Capt'n."*

"I will speak to Kirk." Mox's fist hit the arm of his chair.

"And I say," the engineer countered grimly, *"what are ye Klingons doing here?"*

"It is not your right to ask questions! This territory is unclaimed." Mox leered into the screen. "What are *you* doing here, *Enterprise?"*

"We're exploring, as per our treaty! We've already notified Starfleet Command of your arrival, so you better explain yerself or hightail it back t' where you belong."

Mox felt the pulsing blood of battle. "Hard words for a ship drifting on auxiliary power."

The human leaned forward. *"Is that a threat, Capt'n Mox?"*

As much as Mox wanted to say yes, and back it up with two disrupter banks of power, he knew he couldn't simply slaughter an entire Starfleet crew. He needed to win an honorable battle. He would have to provoke the humans into making a threatening move.

"We detected an energy pulse of immeasurable power," Mox stated flatly. "It originated here, and penetrated Klingon territory. Clearly *that* is a threat to our security. So tell me, engineer, what caused that energy pulse?"

Scott's expression hardly changed. *"Energy pulse? Now yer just making excuses, Klingon. We haven't detected any energy pulse."*

Mox was certain he was lying. Who would tell the truth in a situation such as this. "Were you attacked? Is that why your engines are off-line?"

"Attacked? No . . . we're realigning our warp coils. Our engines will be back on-line soon enough, ye can rest assured of that."

Mox glanced at his first officer, making a slight motion with one hand. Gulda instantly terminated transmission. She kept her eyes on him as he considered the possibilities.

"What are they hiding?" she asked.

"They are hiding Captain Kirk," Mox replied. "That is their weakness."

Gulda turned to her panel, amplifying the scanners. "Our sensors can't penetrate their shields."

Mox considered the fist-sized disc on the screen. "Scan the planet."

While his warriors worked, Mox thought it was revealing that the *Enterprise* didn't hail them again. Starfleet officers were notoriously chatty. Always wanting to talk rather than fight. The flagship was indeed hiding something.

"Captain!" Gulda grinned, showing her jutting bottom teeth as she looked up. "I'm reading a slight ion diffusion on the surface of the planet. It barely registers, but it has the signs of a cloaking shield. Something must be down here."

Mox clenched the arms of his chair. He had longed for days to strike out at someone, to remake his life with his gloved fists. "I will take this victory in the name of my father, Sowron!"

His voice rang out, and it was a measure of their position of power that his crew let out a resounding battle cry. Their eagerness came from all the wrong reasons. But it was enough that they were ready to destroy the Starfleet ship.

Mox knew his eyes burned as he swung toward the screen. "Hail the engineer of the *Enterprise*."

When the pale-skinned, scrawny human appeared on the screen, he was standing, tense, behind his navigator. *"I'm warnin' ye, Mox—ye have no business being in this sector!"*

Mox let his fury flow freely. "You are concealing a weapon on that planet! We have found your cloaking device. You will surrender the weapon at once, or I will consider it a violation of the Organian treaty."

The human reacted as vehemently as Mox could have wished. *"You keep away from here, Klingon!"*

Over his shoulder, Mox ordered, "Close in on the planet. Prepare to transport a security team to the surface." He looked back at the human. "If you will not surrender the weapon, then we are forced to defend ourselves."

Scotty knew the situation was slipping wildly out of control. Captain Mox was spoiling for a fight. The *Enterprise* only had impulse engines operating, providing limited phaser power. Their shields were at a bare sixty-two percent under auxiliary power.

"You don't want to go startin' a galactic incident," Scotty warned. He returned to the chair, hoping to try to calm things down and defuse the situation. "Chargin' in here with disruptor banks armed is not—"

"If you will not surrender the weapon, I will take it from you. Prepare to transport to the surface." Mox was one of the meanest, dirtiest Klingons Scotty

had ever seen—and he had seen a few of the nastier ones.

Lieutenant Radha sent a report straight to the arm-screen of the command chair. The Klingons had locked on to coordinates right next to the entrance to the Kalandan station. His shield had failed—after he had personally assured the captain that it would hold.

"You will not defy me!" Mox bellowed.

The transmission abruptly ended, and Mox disappeared.

"Red alert!" Scotty announced. He knew that wouldn't help the damaged systems.

Lieutenant Radha was calm, as usual. "Sir, the *'Ong* is closing to three hundred thousand kilometers."

"Prepare evasive maneuvers."

Chekov acknowledged and faced the screen with tight shoulders. The Klingon cruiser approached and prepared to enter orbit. Their intent was clear—they were planning to take the planetoid.

"Let's see if we can keep them from entering orbit." Scotty ordered, "Fire a warning shot across their bow."

The intake of breath broke the hush, but no one protested. Scott wasn't sure it was the right thing to do, but he had to try something. Captain Kirk and the landing party were holed up down there with nowhere to run!

"Firing phaser bank, sir," Radha announced.

One bolt of blue phaser-fire lanced through space just in front of the Klingon cruiser. The brightness lit up the bridge.

"Engaging evasive maneuvers," Chekov reported.

The curve of the planetoid swung away as the *Enterprise* changed orbit.

Before they could get around the curve of the planetoid, the *Enterprise* was jolted by return disruptor fire from the Klingon cruiser. "Direct hit to our aft shields," Radha reported. "Shields down to fifty-eight percent."

Scotty held on, hoping the Klingons would be satisfied with one exchange, but the jolting came again and again.

"More direct hits to our aft and port shields," Radha called out. The red-alert sirens were blaring and the power flickered uncertainly. "Shields down to forty-one percent."

"I said evasive maneuvers, Ensign!" Scotty shouted at Chekov. "Get us out of here!"

"All we've got is impulse, sir." Chekov hunched over and braced himself against the navigational controls as another solid impact shook the ship.

"Fire phasers!" Scotty ordered.

Radha could hardly input the commands, the ship was shaking so hard from the quick succession of direct disruptor hits. They could see the jolt of their own phasers against the cruiser, sending a burst of dispelled energy into the surrounding space.

"Direct phaser hit on their starboard shield. No damage!" Rahda called out.

Now there were shouts from the other stations as damage reports flooded in. The lights were flickering and getting weaker.

Another shudder shook the ship as the *Enterprise* finally slipped around the edge of the planetoid.

"The Klingon's gone berserk!" Scotty exclaimed.

"They're coming around!" Radha announced. "Shields at nine percent . . ."

Scotty braced himself. So this was it. He knew Kirk

would never surrender, but he couldn't let this crazy Klingon destroy the thing he loved most in life—the *Enterprise*. He couldn't bear to let her go down in a fight like this.

"Open all channels!" he ordered Lt. Uhura. "Transmit our surrender to the Kling—"

"Sir!" Radha interrupted, her dark eyes astonished. "There's another ship!"

Chapter Seven

TIMING IS EVERYTHING, Tasm reminded herself. She had used the time they spent behind the nebula to absorb every bit of information Kirk relayed to his ship about the Kalandans. It would give her the edge she needed in this engagement.

Just as the new vessel appeared on the edge of the sector, Marl had finally located a neutralizer for the virus. Their database held records of a similar sporophyte virus from the Gooha system in the Beta Quadrant. Marl was already bio-replicating the enzyme that would serve as a catalyst in the removal of certain necessary C-cells that allowed the release of the spores. The active female spores died within a matter of crons, and unless the virus was allowed to release more female spores, there would be nothing to activate the inert male fragments within the gamma globulin molecules. The inert spores were harmless, and would eventually be flushed from their systems. The virus itself could be removed from their tissue using a standard transporter biofilter. Marl's lab team was fast on their way to having a vaccine that would temporarily inhibit the production of C-cells in their glandular tissue.

The arrival of another vessel complicated her plan, so Tasm watched carefully while staying concealed behind the nebula. The exchange between the Klingon and the human was heated. She was the only Petraw who saw it, while the others were quietly absorbed in monitoring systems of their scout ship.

Standing at the subspace station on one side of the small control booth, there was nothing to indicate that Tasm was in complete control of what happened on their ship. It was enough that the others knew, when an order from her appeared on their panels, they were to execute the function without comment.

The Petraw scout ship was on full alert. They could go to faster-than-light and arrive at the planetoid in less than three crons. That gave her plan a nice flexibility.

As the two ships engaged in an overt territorial display, Tasm called up the data on Klingons. The entries were unanimous, with a number of Petraw ships having encountered this species. Klingons were extremely aggressive and disdained any form of cooperation as a weakness. Petraw defenders usually dealt with Klingons, not scouts like themselves.

So their target remained the same—the officers of the *Enterprise.*

Because of the information she had absorbed on the Klingons, Tasm was not surprised when shots were fired.

Tasm pressed the sequence that engaged the engines of the scout ship.

Navigation was already keyed to the coordinates of

the planetoid, and their two new quantum torpedoes were armed. Control of the targeting mechanism was routed to Tasm's panel. They had recently acquired the quantum technology through contact with a people known as the Kikmu. Visiting the icy Kikmu planet had been novel and interesting. In her experience, it was the first time that the other species in an engagement appeared to be as happy with what they got as the Petraw were. But the Kikmu never did find out who they were dealing with.

Though the scout ship was rapidly nearing the battle zone, Tasm was distracted for a moment by a movement of Luz's head. She was standing at the post next to Tasm, controlling navigation. Her lovely Kalandan face grimaced as she stared straight ahead in thought.

Tasm could tell Luz was preoccupied. "Keep your attention on your panel, Luz."

The other two looked up, surprised by the break in their customary silence. When they saw Tasm concentrating on her readouts, they shifted their eyes obediently back to their own panels.

Two crons to go and they would reach the planetoid. The *Enterprise* was much larger than the *'Ong*, but it appeared to wallow in space, rapidly losing power. In its damaged state, it hardly had a chance to defend itself from the punishing disruptor blows. Clearly the Klingons intended to destroy the starship.

When the Klingons didn't react to their approach, Tasm pushed the delay button on the targeting computer. They were entering maximum range, but she intended to take full advantage of the element of surprise.

As the scout ship reached minimum range, the targeting computer automatically released the first quantum torpedo. At the last moment, the Klingon ship veered off at the approach of the Petraw, but it was too late. The quantum torpedo had its own targeting nodes, which led it straight to its intended victim. That was a useful piece of technology they had acquired. Most shields weren't calibrated to resist the innovative quantum weapon.

The Klingon cruiser was flung away from the planetoid by the quantum explosion, and began spinning helplessly.

When the *'Ong* slowly came to rest, sensors indicated that half of one warp nacelle had been blown away. Since the nacelle was joined to the body of the ship, it had also torn off part of the hull.

The communications array revealed that the *Enterprise* was trying to hail them. The starship was also trying to slip around the planetoid, apparently convinced they were the next target. They were, but not in the same way.

The Klingons had not yet reacted. The Petraw scout ship swung around them, nearly matching the cruiser in size.

Suddenly, bright green disruptor beams shot out from the Klingon cruiser. The Petraw scout ship shuddered under the impact. Their shields were more than adequate to deflect the directed energy of a phase disruptor.

Tasm carefully considered what to do next that would enhance and further her plan of engagement.

Deliberately, she keyed the sequence on the second quantum torpedo to target the cruiser's matter/antimatter containment field. The quantum torpedo would punch through the hull and disrupt the field, which would in turn disintegrate the cruiser.

Luz looked up from her panel as the tactical information scrolled by. "But that will kill everyone on board!"

Tasm finished her instructions to the tactical computer. Then she looked up at Luz. "Total destruction is the intended result."

Luz almost retreated into silence, but she couldn't seem to restrain herself. "But why? You could have let the Klingons destroy the *Enterprise* and fight the men in the station before finishing them off!"

Their other pod-mates in the command booth—Kad and Marl—were staring now with open mouths. Luz had made a spectacle of herself before, but never in the tricky opening sequence of an engagement. None of them questioned their leader.

"I may have to remove you from this engagement," Tasm said flatly.

Luz immediately busied herself with her panel, apparently shaken by the threat. Tasm knew that Luz was different from her other pod-mates, but her passion for engagements couldn't be questioned. Her fitness to perform would have to be evaluated later, not in the heat of battle.

The Klingons directed two more blasts from their disruptors at the Petraw ship, which bounced harmlessly off their shields. The *Enterprise* was still trying to hail them.

Tasm pressed the command for the tactical computer to proceed. The quantum torpedo launched and homed in on the Klingon cruiser.

The *'Ong* lurched as the explosion ripped through its side. Then a huge cloud of orange sparks mushroomed out, larger, then larger still, engulfing itself with successive waves of expanding energy.

The advance shock wave hit the Petraw scout ship, knocking it from its course. Tasm was occupied while they regained control of the ship, but she did take a moment's satisfaction in the good start to their engagement. Now the *Enterprise* would be beholden to them, and their guise of being the descendants of the all-powerful Kalandans would be reinforced. A touch of fear never hurt during negotiations, as long as that fear was properly channeled.

Lt. Uhura couldn't move when she saw the torpedo from the unidentified ship zeroing in on the Klingon cruiser. Chekov shouted, "It's going to hit!" just as the torpedo impacted.

Everyone on the bridge winced in sympathy at the explosion. The *Enterprise* was moving too slowly for comfort as they tried to get behind the planetoid. They were rocked by the shock wave.

On the screen, the sparks faded, leaving no sign of wreckage. The Klingon cruiser and all on board were simply gone.

It was so unexpected. The *Enterprise*'s shields were failing and they were about to be destroyed . . . the next thing Uhura knew, this strange ship was swooping in to annihilate the Klingons!

"What *was* that weapon?" Scotty demanded.

Second Science Officer Momita, a fleshy Tau Ceti female, was frantically trying to analyze the science readings. "The initial explosion was caused by some sort of quantum-level discharge. A warp-core breech finished them off."

"Quantum torpedo . . ." Scotty sounded impressed. "I dinna know they really existed."

"It sure packs a punch," Chekov agreed.

Feeling numb, Uhura automatically continued to try to hail the unidentified ship. Scotty was chewing his bottom lip, staring at the screen. He looked like he was wondering if the *Enterprise* was next.

"No answer to our hails, Mr. Scott," Uhura reported, trying to keep her voice from wavering. "Damage reports coming in from all decks."

"Aye . . ." Scotty checked the reports on his arm console. Much of the damage was from overloaded secondary systems as the shields failed. The ship had been in bad shape before the pounding of the Klingon disruptor fire.

Uhura was almost surprised when the unknown ship refrained from circling around and attacking them. Instead, it entered orbit around the planetoid.

"Pull back a bit," Scotty ordered Chekov, who seemed happy to comply.

Scotty abandoned his chair console and joined Momita at the science station. "Have ye got an identification on that vessel, Mo?"

Momita's usual grin was twisted now in concern. "Negative, sir. Sensors indicate the ship has been extensively modified on successive occasions."

The image on screen magnified, and Uhura finally got a good look at the ship. It had an unusual silhouette. What appeared to be warp nacelles were attached directly to the body of the ship. The cylindrical hull bulged mysteriously in several places from large attached components. Blocks of the original brick-red enamel had been repainted in shades ranging from brown to orange. A bristle of arrays capped off the front end, making it look like a stinging insect—something malformed and deadly.

"Who *are* they?" Scotty voiced the question on everyone's mind.

"They're no friends of the Klingons, that's for sure," Chekov said.

Momita examined her computer screen. "The ship is similar in some ways to a Denevian vessel encountered by the Starfleet scout ship *Crockett* when it was exploring on the border of the Beta Quadrant. There isn't much information on the Denevians, but they certainly weren't this well-armed."

The imminent threat posed by an unidentified ship—it felt like one of those unlikely Starfleet Academy exercises, only this one was real. Uhura wondered how many of the other bridge officers were thinking about Captain Kirk and what he would do in this situation.

Uhura took the liberty of switching from their automatic hail to her own voice. Sometimes the personal touch made all the difference, and this certainly seemed like one of those times to try anything. "This is the *Starship Enterprise* of the United Federation of Planets. Unidentified vessel, please respond."

After a few quiet repetitions, Uhura finally got a return signal. "Sir! They're responding."

Scotty nodded, turning from where he stood at the science station. "On screen, Lieutenant."

Everyone looked to see who had just blown away a Klingon ship.

A woman's head and shoulders appeared. She looked familiar, and for a moment Uhura felt relief. She had dark slanted brows like Mr. Spock's, over brightly colored eyelids.

"I am Tasm, commander of this ship." Her serene smile was a bit jarring for someone who had just mur-

dered a hundred sentient beings. *"We are from the Ka-landan colony Beta-nine."*

Uhura gasped. That's who she looked like—Losira! The ancient commander who had left such a tender, touching message for her people.

Uhura could see the resemblance, though Commander Tasm's face was flatter, not so regal in expression. Her uniform was also different, darker and concealing her upper body below her neck.

Scotty seemed similarly taken aback. "Kalandans, did you say?"

"Yes." Her perfect mouth carefully formed the words. *"This is our science station."*

Uhura slowly removed her earpiece. With the communication on screen, she didn't need it. Everything was beginning to make sense.

"We are not receiving an answer from the station. Is that your shield over the entrance?" Tasm never took her eyes off Scotty.

Uhura knew Scotty must be cursing inside. He had been so convinced that his portable shield would conceal the landing party. He would probably spend the next three months in his quarters trying to perfect the unit.

After a few moments, Scotty evasively retorted, "You'll pardon me for asking, but I thought you people were dead!"

Tasm smiled slightly. *"No, my people are quite well. But we lost contact with our advance force many millennia ago. We had believed this station was destroyed. Our colony in the Beta Quadrant just detected an energy signal that alerted us to its location."*

"You weren't the first," Scotty pointed out. "Why'd

you have to destroy that Klingon cruiser? They were no threat to you."

"It appeared they were about to destroy you. We've found that Klingons are an aggressive, warlike race who are resistant to cooperation. I was forced to take action to protect our property."

Scotty was getting tense again. *No wonder,* Uhura thought, *these Kalandans are remarkably cavalier.* And Tasm was certainly building a case for kicking off every Starfleet officer who was trespassing on the station.

"Now hold on there, Commander," Scotty drawled. "Starfleet has possession of this station by right of salvage."

"If we hadn't arrived, the Klingons would now be in possession of both this station and your ship. Consider it a mutually beneficial trade. You keep your ship while we take our station back."

Scotty hesitated. In their weakened state, there was no possible way the *Enterprise* could fight the Kalandan ship. But their orders were clear—Starfleet Command wanted to know more about the Kalandan technology.

"Some of our officers *can't* get back to the ship," Scotty finally admitted. "There's some kind of disease on the station."

"The sporophyte virus?" Tasm blandly smiled. *"You might want to tell your captain that we have the vaccine."*

That got Scotty's attention. "Vaccine? You mean you can cure it?"

"Notify your captain that we are prepared to transport down to the station with the vaccine for the virus."

The Kalandans closed the channel, then Uhura closed it from their end. "Communication terminated," she reported.

Scotty took a deep breath. "Almost too good t' be true," he murmured.

Uhura was puzzled by his reaction, but she would never say so out loud. It seemed like the most natural thing in the galaxy that the mighty Kalandan people would know when their station had been reactivated. Finding such an ancient piece of their own history would also make them quick to eliminate any threat, as the Klingons obviously were. Still . . . all those people killed for no apparent reason . . .

Scotty turned to Uhura, his expression serious. "Get me the captain."

Chapter Eight

KIRK WAS EXPECTING Scotty's hail, but he wasn't expecting to hear that the Klingons had attacked the *Enterprise*—then had been ambushed and destroyed by a Kalandan vessel.

"They want the station back, Captain," Scotty informed him. *"And the* Enterprise *is in no condition t' stop them. They have quantum torpedoes. . . ."* he finished in a reverent tone.

Kirk glanced down at the open container filled with Kalandan personal effects. He had seen ample evidence of the Kalandan's power. Yet he was also getting to know them as people. They kept such frivolous mementos of their travels, especially the beautiful plant specimens encased in clear carbonite spheres and octagons. Some of the organic-based souvenirs disintegrated in a puff of dust when he touched them. The nonorganic plaster figurines and calcified shells had survived.

Among the belongings he had searched there were

hundreds of the round computer interface cards. But he found no slots to feed them into.

Kirk knew they were at a standstill. He heard the tension in Scotty's voice, and could only imagine what his crew was going through up there. It was time to break this stalemate.

"I'm not going to hand over this station," Kirk said. "Not even exchange for the vaccine to the virus."

Scotty sounded calmer now that Kirk was making the decisions. *"Then what, sir?"*

"Contact their commander. Tell her that Dr. McCoy and I will meet her on the surface of the station, near the entrance." One of the advantages he most appreciated about Scotty's shield was that they could step through from the inside without turning it off. The downside was that he wouldn't be able to get back in again.

"Aye, sir!" Scotty agreed. *"When?"*

Kirk picked up a small carved stone from the container in front of him. He held it in his fist for a moment, then slipped it into his pocket. "Do it now."

Kirk gathered the landing party in the upper chamber, where the destroyed computer node had managed to baffle Spock. "McCoy, you're with me. We'll see what kind of medical technicians these Kalandans are."

"I'd like to find out how they cured this virus." McCoy eagerly slung his medical tricorder over one shoulder.

Kirk opened his communicator when it beeped. "Yes, Scotty?"

"Commander Tasm is on her way down, along with two crew members, sir."

"What's the status on the repairs?" Kirk asked.

Scotty sounded more subdued. *"We were almost through with th' repairs, but the Klingons did a job on th' ship, that they did. We'll not be able to power up warp engines for another few hours, Captain. Auxiliary power is holding, but th' shields are barely at thirty-five percent."*

"Get warp power back on-line," Kirk ordered. That was a priority. "Keep a channel open to Spock. Under no circumstances allow anyone to transport down to the surface. Understood?"

"Aye, sir!"

When the rock slab slid aside, the planetoid looked exactly the same as before. Kirk could see perfectly well through the shield.

The sky hardly changed with the passage of time, staying the same murky purplish-pink. It looked very different from the scene the Losira replica had showed them in the control room. There was nothing left of the clinging, flowering vines or the tall, willowy tree-ferns. Now it was stark and silent, with only the stunted shocks of yellow grass left alive.

"They aren't here yet," McCoy commented. "They must plan on making an entrance."

The rock slab slid shut behind them, pushing Kirk against the shield.

Nervously, McCoy eyed the shield inches away from his nose. A static spark leaped from the brush of his finger against it. "I'm as big a fan of Scotty's work as anyone . . . but this is his baby. His judgment about it may be a bit skewed."

"It gives us one more barrier between the station and everyone else."

"Yeah, but what if it electrocutes us?"

Kirk sighed and stepped through. There was an unpleasant play of static electricity against his skin, but it didn't hurt.

McCoy grimaced as he pushed through the shield. He settled his uniform jacket without saying anything.

From somewhere nearby, there was the high-pitched whine of a transporter. Kirk and McCoy started toward the edge of the clearing. They could hear the crunch of footsteps approaching.

Three humanoids appeared from behind a rocky outcropping. Kirk's first thought was that these Kalandans were smaller than Losira. But as they approached, he realized he could look them in the eye, just like the Losira replica. They seemed smaller because they were much more slender.

"I am Commander Tasm from the Kalandan colony Beta-nine." The center female gestured to the man and woman on either side of her. "These are my officers: Kad, my second-in-command, and Luz, our medical technician."

Kirk introduced himself and Dr. McCoy, while taking a good look at the Kalandans. They didn't have the striking presence that Losira had. Their faces were slightly flattened, with rather small features. They wore dark purple uniforms that completely covered them from their toes to the base of their neck. After Losira's minimalist, midriff-revealing uniform, the effect was stifling.

But one look into Tasm's eyes revealed the resemblance. It was disturbing when he remembered how Losira had killed three of his men. Tasm had just killed a hundred Klingons.

Commander Tasm was smiling slightly as she continued past Kirk and McCoy, going straight to the rock slab concealing the doorway. "Please deactivate your shield so we may enter the station."

So she knew exactly where the door was. It had taken his team an entire day to track it down.

"Not so fast." Kirk stood behind her, arms crossed. He waited until she turned to face him. "We haven't discussed the ownership of this station yet."

"Yes, I can see that is your concern. Luz, the vaccine." Tasm made a slight gesture to her medical officer.

Luz was shorter and just as thin as Tasm. Whereas Tasm had a confident, regal manner, Luz seemed more relaxed. She pulled a cylindrical medical instrument from her pouch and passed it over to her commander. When she glanced at Kirk, he noticed her eyelids were green and blue, whereas Tasm had yellow and orange stripes over her eyes.

Tasm handed Kirk the device. "This contains the vaccine for the sporophyte virus. It is a temporary inhibitor, so it must be taken every day. We do not recommend you take it for more than several days in a row."

McCoy aimed his medical tricorder at the device. "C-cell suppressor . . . I see . . ." He quickly absorbed the information. "Yes! That would halt the production of the active spores. With their short life-cycle, yes, it would work!" McCoy turned to Kirk, relieved. "Why didn't I think of that?"

"Can we test it?" Kirk asked.

Tasm handed over the device. "Take a dose of the vaccine. It works quickly to halt spore production."

"The transporter biofilter will remove the virus itself

from our tissue." McCoy took the device from Kirk, running another scan. "It's got nothing harmful to us in it. I'll try it first."

The medical officer stepped forward to show him how to operate the medical device. Luz smiled at McCoy in a shy way. Kirk noticed that Bones managed to catch her eyes to return the smile. She administered the vaccine much like a hypospray. From the doctor's expression, he felt nothing.

McCoy scanned himself with the handheld medical scanner. "It's taking effect. It's not a real cure, but it gives us enough protection to leave this place without infecting the rest of the crew."

Tasm was looking around. "This station must be thoroughly decontaminated before it can be reoccupied by my people. We've been ordered to accompany the station back to our colony in the Beta Quadrant. It's a remarkable discovery for my people." She paused to let that sink in. "Other vessels have been dispatched to assist us."

Kirk merely said, "Give me the vaccine, Bones." He waited until McCoy had administered a dose of the vaccine. "Can you replicate it for the rest of the landing party?"

"All I need is the ship's bio-replicator," McCoy assured him. "Now that I know what it takes to suppress the spore production, we can make our own."

Tasm remained perfectly poised in front of the doorway. "So you have what you want. Now please return our station to us."

Kirk tilted his head as if considering it. "By rights of salvage—"

"Yes, we know that you have laws about possession;

however, those are not *our* laws. The fact is, this station belongs to my people. Some of our ancient technology can be used in a dangerous and harmful way, and we must protect it."

"We've had a dose of that ourselves." He held her gaze. "The defense computer killed three of my men, using cellular disruption."

"I am truly sorry. Our ancestors were capable of terrible feats, which have mercifully been lost in time." Her head inclined slightly. "You agree then that we must take custody of this station for the protection of innocent others."

Kirk didn't quite know what to say. It was Starfleet's orders that he prevent this technology from falling into enemy hands. If the vaccine worked, nothing would be easier than to take his officers back to the *Enterprise* and let the Kalandans protect the station when Klingon reinforcements arrived. But the easy way wasn't necessarily the right way.

"We found this station and are in possession of it. Can you prove it really belongs to your people?"

Only Tasm's lips moved. "This station was created ten thousand years ago. Much of our ancient history was lost in the intervening dark age."

"So you don't have the capability to transport across light-years? Or cause cellular disruption?"

"No, those technological advances have been lost. Our people once used dimensional transporters to travel between our colonies."

"But you must be able to tell me *something* about this station," Kirk protested.

Regretfully Tasm glanced around. "We do know this particular station was under the command of Losira. It was lost at the start of the plague-era, when the sporo-phyte virus devastated our empire. Historians have long believed that had something to do with why we lost contact with this station."

It sounded about right to Kirk. "Do you know what the station is like inside? Do you have blueprints of the place?"

"No blueprints, which is why this is such a remark-able event." Her two officers were now looking more excited. "We do know there is a command center some levels down, with an interactive computer-replica of the station's commander."

McCoy made a small noise, as if that was enough to convince him. Kirk had to agree. He almost reached for his communicator to tell Scotty to deactivate the shield.

But something wasn't right. He couldn't pinpoint it, but this commander was a tad smooth for his taste. She watched him too carefully.

"I'd like to consult Starfleet Command about your request." Kirk wasn't sure where the words came from. He rarely if ever brought Starfleet Command into his decisions. But a gut feeling told him that he needed time.

A spasm of frustration briefly distorted her beautiful face, then she was serene again. "If you do not have the authority yourself . . ."

Kirk knew that was meant to be a taunt, so he didn't react. "Dr. McCoy, when can we try transporting back to the ship?"

McCoy scanned both himself and Kirk again, check-ing his readings against the medical tricorder. "We should be able to transport up now. The inert spore fragments have nothing to activate them to grow new viruses."

It was a test, but the risk was small. If Commander Tasm wanted to destroy his crew, she could do it with one quantum torpedo.

Tasm held out one hand, the first time she had reached out. He had a flash of Losira doing the same thing, with the same urgency in her eyes.

"If you won't let us inside the station, then take us to your ship. Let me talk to your commanding officer."

Kirk hesitated as he opened his communicator. But it was the first request that he felt comfortable with. "Agreed." He tuned in to the ship's frequency. "Scotty, Kirk here. We have five to beam up. Two human and three Kalandan."

"Aye, sir," was Scotty's dour reply.

As they dematerialized from the station, Tasm considered the first direct exchange of their engagement to be a success. The Starfleet officers were beholden to them, which was the preferred way to start. And she had almost convinced the captain on the spot that the station rightfully belonged to them.

Playing out the character was her only course of action. It would take another mega-cron to finish replicating new quantum torpedoes. Without the torpedoes, their laser weapons couldn't pierce the *Enterprise* shields. And that still left the Starfleet officers ensconced in the station. The Petraw numbered twelve, while the *Enterprise* had hundreds of crew members who would risk their lives to defend their fellow officers. Besides, Tasm was a scout, not a defender. Scouts only fought when victory was assured.

Her only concern was Luz. After her pod-mate's outburst in the command booth, Tasm wouldn't have brought Luz down to the surface except that the engineer said their doctor would accompany the captain. Tasm had seriously considered reassigning Luz's target to Mlan. But everything was moving too quickly to change, and now she was committed. She would have to rely on the character Luz had developed.

When they materialized on board the *Enterprise,* the two Starfleet officers let out almost imperceptible sighs of relief.

"You made it, Captain!" The crew member at the transporter controls couldn't restrain his burst of enthusiasm. Tasm would have disciplined any of her crew who revealed so much. "The virus has been removed from you both."

The doctor seemed very pleased to be back on board their starship. Their gratitude would build quickly now. Not only was their ship saved, but their key officers were no longer trapped on the station.

Tasm was the embodiment of composure, as she took the opportunity to gather more information about Starfleet for the Petraw. The *Enterprise* was a remarkable ship, at least four times bigger than the biggest Petraw scout ships. The spaciousness was immediately noticeable. An entire chamber was allotted just for the use of the transporters.

"So the vaccine worked." Kirk inclined his head toward Tasm.

"As I told you it would." Tasm contented herself with a casual glance about the transporter room. Later she would explore more thoroughly. She wanted to get a good look at those pattern buffers—there might be something the Petraw could use there.

"I'm going to replicate the vaccine for the landing party," McCoy informed his captain.

Tasm took the opportunity to say, "Officer Luz could accompany you and assist, if needed."

McCoy hesitated, but his eyes lingered on Luz, who was starting to smile and nod at him. "Sure . . . Captain?"

Kirk frowned slightly, but waved them away. "Keep me posted."

Tasm gave Luz's effort a satisfactory review thus far. She was taking the demure route, while paying complete attention to the doctor. It was best not to be overtly coy or alluring—the fascination level should not peak before they got what they needed. Besides, the Kalandans were scientists, and above all they must stay in character.

Kirk turned to Tasm and Kad. "This way."

Tasm followed the captain out of the transporter room into a wide corridor. It didn't have components in the walls like their own ship. It was also much brighter and bigger, with numerous doors leading into chambers even larger than the transporter room.

Kirk stepped into a small nook and held on to one of the handles. "Conference room," he said out loud. Tasm lurched slightly as it moved. Some kind of internal transport. She briefly wondered what it would be like to travel through space in such an enormous vessel. It was too ostentatious for her taste, and would undoubtedly attract a great deal of attention, which was unsafe.

Kirk took something from his pants pocket. "Here, take a look at this."

Tasm took the small, rounded object. It felt heavy, like a rock, and was gray, but it was smoothed and polished. On both ends it was incised with curving lines. "What is it?"

"I was hoping you could tell me," Kirk said. "I found it on the station."

Tasm knew better than to claim knowledge she didn't have. It was one of the quickest ways to tip off a target. "I haven't seen anything similar. Where did you find it?"

"In one of the living quarters."

Tasm was surprised. The last message she had intercepted from Kirk to his ship had said nothing about locating living quarters. She thought he was still stuck in the command center.

When everything else failed, rely on character. Tasm lifted the tiny object to let the light shine off it. "I long to see the station. It's like the past come alive. . . ."

Kirk finally smiled with genuine warmth. That's when she knew she was playing it too aloof. He clearly felt more comfortable with a woman who was accessible. She had already proven their technological superiority, perhaps now it was time for the soft touch.

"It is a remarkable place," Kirk agreed.

Tasm let her smile deepen. "Then hurry with your consultation so we can return to the station."

The doorway opened and Kirk led them toward another vast room, this one with a long trapezoidal table. He asked them to wait there and left them alone. There was no one guarding the door. They were almost completely trusted. Soon she would be in the Kalandan station.

All she needed was a few words with the Losira replica and she was certain she could find the technology they were looking for. Kirk had it wrong, thinking the Kalandans were a defensive people. They weren't. They had just created a defense computer that was very efficient at its job. Tasm had met a lot of different aliens, and she was sure the Kalandans were ready and waiting to bend over backward to help them. So many people were in this galaxy. All she needed was one chance.

Chapter Nine

SULU WAITED ANXIOUSLY inside the station during Captain Kirk's negotiation with the newly arrived Kalandans. He expected any moment to see the door breached and the landing party forced to defend their position. His post was inside the corridor leading to the botany labs, which was designated their fall-back route. Since it was lined by interlocking science labs, it would serve as an ideal warren for a defensive counterattack.

Sulu's grip on his phaser, set for stun, was tight as the minutes ticked by. Spock looked impassive and cool as usual, but Reinhart was sweating from nerves.

When Spock was finally notified that Captain Kirk and Dr. McCoy had successfully beamed up to the *Enterprise* with their Kalandan guests, Sulu realized the worst was over. It looked like they finally had a way to purge the toxic virus from their bodies. And now that the Kalandan commander and her officers were onboard the *Enterprise,* surely there would be no hostile move made against the station.

But Spock maintained his defensive position behind the lift in the entrance chamber. He was seated on the portable stool, his phaser out and aimed at the entryway to the station.

Sulu hesitated, then said from his post, "So that's that. Now we wait to hear back from the captain."

Reinhart uncertainly held his position near the door. As security, Reinhart had taken the first line of defense.

Spock kept watching the entryway, his communicator in front of him with the channel to the *Enterprise* open.

Sulu waited a few moments, but he was keyed up from the adrenaline rush of facing an all-out invasion that hadn't occurred. Finally he said, "Sir, request permission to resume searching the Kalandan living quarters."

Spock lifted one brow at him, then glanced at Reinhart, who came forward a couple of steps. "Very well, Mr. Sulu," Spock said. "You and Reinhart may proceed. Maintain communicator contact. If there is any disturbance, you will return here immediately."

"Understood," Sulu acknowledged. He jerked his head for Reinhart to come along.

Sulu was relieved to not have to stay in the entrance chamber, on constant alert against an attack. But when he was again confronted by the dozens of corridors and hundreds of chambers, he was daunted by the task ahead. Most of the things they had discovered were of no immediate value. Spock had theorized that while the colony itself appeared to be ten thousand years old, the civilization itself was much older and showed signs of millennia of development.

Sulu stayed near the quarters closest to the doorway to the botany labs. "Why not start here?" he suggested. "That way we're closer to the entrance chamber."

Reinhart looked as if, on second thought, he wasn't relishing looking through more private effects of long-dead Kalandans. "It's almost not right," he protested, stepping into the next chamber.

Sulu wanted to agree when he saw this one. Unlike the others, this chamber was not stripped and packed neatly into clear containers. It looked as if the scientist living here had stumbled up from sleep and staggered out the door, never to return again.

He stepped carefully over the threshold. There were several white containers of petrified substance on the ledge next to the door. It looked like a science experiment gone bad, or ten-thousand-year-old leftovers. Clothing was strewn on the floor and draped across the sofa-bench—mostly narrow strips of material edged with metallic thread.

Other stuff had been left where it was thrown, styluses, measuring devices, and stacks of magnetic film that had apparently been used for taking notes. Now they were blank, and none recorded a mark when Sulu tried to press a stylus against them.

"Maybe the components have failed," Sulu ventured a guess.

"What's this?" Reinhart asked, holding up a round flat disc about three centimeters across. It was split into quarters colored yellow and red.

Sulu shrugged, his eyes widening. "Who knows?

Look at all this stuff! There's got to be a station map or *something* in here."

But after thoroughly riffling through the contents of the room, they found lots of things they didn't recognize but nothing that looked like a map. They did gather up dozens more of the round plastic computer interfaces. But there were no appropriate slots on any of the devices they found.

Frustrated, Sulu sat down on the bed. "This is impossible."

Reinhart shifted uneasily, putting down some of the loose bits of stuff they had found. "At least it's clean. You should see the dust on my shelves."

"It *is* clean." Sulu looked around sharply. "Why didn't I think about that before?"

"Because the other rooms had the stuff packed up," Reinhart said reasonably.

"You're right. Everything in this room was left lying around. Yet there's still no dust . . . not here, and not in the botany labs."

Sulu aimed his tricorder at the clothes left on the floor. But there were no signs of humanoid tissue—not a skin flake or hair was left. Even the ancient science stuff bore no defining characteristics, with the organic matter long since decayed.

"This station must have a good ventilation system," Sulu said. "It's scoured this place clean." He got up and began examining the walls, looking for a vent of some kind.

Reinhart looked surprised, then he nodded. "The air *is* fresh in here."

"If I'm right . . ." Sulu bent over to look under a ledge that served as a table. "Ah-ha! There it is."

Reinhart also bent down to see the narrow strip that ran just under the ledge. It was a grid of tiny holes.

"A vent," Reinhart said, sounding puzzled. "But it's hardly as wide as my hand. There's no way we can get through that."

"That's right." Sulu remembered what Spock had done with the monofilaments in the computer node. "But I know something that can."

Sulu was on his way back to the entrance chamber when Spock checked in with him via communicator. There was no news yet from the *Enterprise*.

So Sulu told Spock his idea about sending nanites into the air vent. By the time Sulu arrived in the entrance chamber, Spock had programmed a vial of nanites.

"I will remain here to track the nanites with the remote operator," Spock told Sulu.

Sulu saluted and ran back the way he had come, carrying the dispenser and vial. If they could give Captain Kirk more information about the station, then he would be in a stronger position to negotiate with the Kalandans.

Reinhart was waiting for his return. Sulu held up the dispenser and went directly to the air vent. He was breathing hard from his jog to and from the entrance chamber. McCoy had warned him that his injured shoulder would take a toll on him for a few more days.

Eagerly, Sulu placed the opening of the dispenser against one of the tiny holes. With one smooth motion, he injected the nanites into the vent.

Sulu opened his communicator and tuned to their landing party station frequency. "They're off, Mr. Spock."

"Acknowledged." Spock didn't sound nearly as excited.

Sulu waited, knowing that the nanites didn't move quickly. He tried to see into the vent, but it was blackness beyond the wall. Each hole looked as if it had been punched into the plasteel, leaving the edges curving inward. Focusing on one hole, moving closer, it seemed to grow larger and larger, as if he could almost see inside. . . .

Sulu abruptly sat back, shaking his head. What a disorienting feeling . . .

"I feel dizzy." Reinhart put one hand to his head, swaying where he sat.

Sulu sagged, holding himself up with one arm. "'S the vent! Somethin's wrong . . ."

He fumbled with the communicator, but it seemed a long way off. Then he slowly crumpled to the floor. Still scrabbling at the communicator, trying to get it close to his mouth, he mumbled, "Mm . . . sss . . ."

Behind him, there was a thud as Reinhart fell off the bed platform. He could still see the room, the curve where the ceiling met the wall, and the recessed lights. But darkness nibbled at the edges, and soon Sulu couldn't see anything.

Captain Kirk sat in his chair on the bridge, once more in command of his ship. The familiar whirs and dings from the control panels were soothing to his ears. Reports were pouring in. The *Enterprise* was quickly being repaired—Scotty had the new integrator in place and a test run of the warp engines would commence soon. After Dr. McCoy replicated the vaccine, the landing party would be able to return to the ship.

But from his vantage point on the bridge of the *Enterprise,* Kirk had a wary feeling about these newly arrived Kalandans. Why did they utterly destroy the Klingon ship the instant they had arrived, only to wait patiently in his conference room to negotiate with him?

What did the *Enterprise* have that the Kalandans wanted? Possession of the station. Since that appeared to be the only leverage they had against the Kalandans, Kirk was reluctant to disengage the shield and hand it over to them.

Kirk sent a report to Starfleet Command purely in an effort to gain time. They needed warp capability in order to stand a chance against Tasm's ship, if it came to a fight. There was nothing they could do to defend themselves against quantum torpedoes except run.

Kirk was in agreement with Tasm on one thing—the Klingons were an "aggressive warlike race who are resistant to cooperation." Captain Mox had confirmed his opinion of the Klingons. In the incident last month, it had taken much bloodshed before Kang had listened to Kirk and Mara. Even then, they had almost failed to forge a cooperative response to reject the malevolent entity.

Mox had appeared to be worse, according to the logs of the incident. They were fortunate the Kalandans had arrived when they did.

Uhura turned, touching one hand to her earpiece. "Captain, Mr. Spock is signaling from the station."

Kirk hit the audio channel. "Yes, Spock?"

"Captain, a defense system was triggered, locking Mr. Sulu and Security Guard Reinhart into one of the living quarters."

"The defense computer is off-line," Kirk protested.

"Apparently, this was a local defense system that was activated after Mr. Sulu injected nanites into a vent. I tracked their progress for one point four-nine meters, where the nanites were destroyed." Spock's tone became dryer still, if that was possible. *"When I received no response from Mr. Sulu, I proceeded to their location. I removed the sealed plasticized osmium door using a phaser set on level five."*

"Good job, Spock."

"Both men were unconscious inside—"

"Spock!" Kirk's finger moved to deactivate the shield around the station, but the landing party couldn't be transported up until they had received the vaccine.

"—and I revived them," Spock finished calmly. *"They are both unharmed. It appears the oxygen was removed from the chamber when the local defense system was activated by the nanites."*

"Well . . ." Kirk said thoughtfully. "Those nanites haven't been much help, have they?"

"Indeed," Spock agreed. *"What information can the Kalandans give us?"*

"Not much," Kirk admitted. "They claim they lost most of their technological advances in their dark ages. Anyway, they say they don't have interstellar transporters or the cellular disruptor."

"Most unusual," Spock commented.

"Yes. I don't like it, Spock."

Kirk waited, but Spock had nothing else to add to his report. Such as it was. "Hold your position," he ordered. "Kirk out."

The channel closed as Kirk's fist softly hit the arm of his command chair. Options were being exhausted on every side. Clearly, the Kalandan station was still a deadly place for his people.

Kirk was wondering when Commander Tasm's patience would end when Dr. McCoy reported that the vaccine was replicated and ready to be administered to the landing party. It would protect them for approximately twenty-two hours; then they would need a booster shot. McCoy agreed with the Kalandans that no one should receive more than two booster shots in a row.

Before Kirk had listened to the entire report, Uhura announced that they were receiving an encoded subspace message from Commodore Enwright at Starfleet Command. Kirk put it on the screen.

Enwright's upper lip was drawn back, as if he didn't like what he had to say. But he said it anyway. *"Starfleet Command authorizes you to extend all courtesy to the Kalandans and proceed with standard diplomatic overtures."*

Apparently Starfleet Command saw the wisdom in befriending a powerful race who wouldn't hesitate to destroy Klingons.

Enwright's tone became firmer. *"Otherwise, your orders remain the same. Acquire information on the ancient Kalandan technology. Do not allow these weapons to fall into enemy hands."*

Enwright's face faded on the screen, leaving a hush in the bridge. It couldn't have been clearer. If the Kalandans were their allies, they could take the station, as long as Kirk got scans of everything they found inside. Basically that was Kirk's opinion of what should be done, except for some niggling instinct inside that cried out *"No!"* He couldn't explain it.

"So," Kirk softly exclaimed. "It looks like we've acquired some new friends. . . ."

"Sir?" Uhura interjected. "I've been decoding the noise at the time the Klingon cruiser *'Ong* was destroyed. I believe I've located a distress signal. The *'Ong* must have sent a message to the Klingon Defense Force, telling them they were under attack."

Startled, Kirk turned to Science Officer Momita. "How long before a Klingon battleship can arrive?"

"Hmm . . ." Momita consulted the computer. "I'd say approximately forty-four hours, if they travel at top warp speed."

Suddenly time was no longer an ally.

Kirk pushed himself out of his chair. Now he needed to see how much the Kalandans would cooperate.

"The Klingon reinforcements are on their way." Kirk told Commander Tasm when they would arrive.

It took a moment for her second-in-command to translate the amount of time into their numbers. Both seemed to relax. "Klingons do not concern us," Tasm said with a private smile.

"Klingons concern *us* a great deal. We have a treaty to maintain with them."

"We do not," Commander Tasm pointed out.

"I suggest a compromise. We will examine the station together. If I'm satisfied that you can protect the station and keep it out of Klingon hands, then in two days' time, we'll be on our way."

Tasm smiled at him. "We will not be dependent on your whim. However, we have no objection to you exploring this station with us. It is a remarkable archeological find."

"More than that," Kirk murmured. But her quiet beauty again reminded him of Losira as she recorded her logs. Tasm had the same alluring confidence. If they had to be allies with someone, he would chose the Kalandans over the Klingons anytime.

Chapter Ten

Luz STILL COULDN'T believe it—Tasm had given away their biggest advantage without getting anything in return! The vaccine for the sporophyte virus was worth everything to those stranded Starfleet officers, and to simply hand it over was unconscionable. Why had they waited in that nebula for so long trying to find the antidote if Tasm intended to just toss it away?

Luz seethed inside while Dr. McCoy whipped up a replica of the sporophyte vaccine. It was galling to think of that idiot Tasm stuck somewhere in this ship, letting Starfleet get the edge on them. If Luz had been in charge of this engagement, they would already be on the surface, taking possession of the station.

It was so unfortunate that she hadn't been on the subspace post at the time their ship detected the message from the *Enterprise*. Then she could have taken over as leader.

Luz had already examined the sickbay on the *Enterprise*. It was surprisingly backward for such a technologically advanced civilization. With one cursory look at the equipment tray and bio-bed, she verified that the devices performed a minimal of biological functions. There was nothing worth acquiring here, as far as medical technology went.

Her target, Dr. McCoy, was also not very stimulating. He was clearly relieved to be back onboard his ship. The other medical technicians broke away from their duties to gather around him, smiling and calling out greetings. But, rather self-consciously, McCoy had introduced Luz as a Kalandan doctor who was providing them with the vaccine for the sporophyte virus. They got to work replicating it.

The medical staff were grateful yet wary of her. Their reaction confirmed her initial opinion. Tasm had made a mistake giving the vaccine to the *Enterprise* crew so readily. It was too easy, and didn't make sense after the way they had blown that Klingon ship away. That had been a glorious move on Tasm's part, but she should have let them finish off the *Enterprise* first. Since that one bold stroke, Tasm had followed up with nothing.

These humans seemed gullible enough to believe they were Kalandans, but clearly a few of them still had some doubts. And that was too bad, because their plan to impersonate Kalandans was basically workable. It was Tasm's handling of the situation that had left them hanging around on this ship when they should be down on the surface examining that station.

McCoy introduced Luz to M'Benga, the doctor who had been in charge of sickbay until McCoy returned. "Are your people always this generous?" M'Benga asked, his expression hiding any doubts he might have.

Luz shrugged one shoulder. "Commander Tasm can be capricious—either very generous or very . . . severe. I'm sure those Klingons would like to exchange places with you right now."

With his smile frozen on his face, M'Benga bowed slightly as he pulled away. Several other technicians heard her reply. Maybe her comment would travel to Captain Kirk's ears. Maybe he would be more cautious of Tasm rather than underestimate them.

If Luz had to, she would single-handedly make this engagement a success.

Once the Starfleet medical technicians had finished replicating the antidote and had loaded it into hyposprays, Dr. McCoy suggested that he take Luz to join Commander Tasm in the conference room. Luz didn't want to sit around doing nothing like Tasm and Kad, so instead she asked for a tour of sickbay.

McCoy clearly had other things on his mind, but was too polite to refuse. "After everything you've done for us . . ."

Luz turned her smile of amusement into something special just for him. He had been trapped on that planetoid for days, and no doubt he wanted to retreat to meditate—or whatever it was humans did to relax.

Before McCoy had finished showing Luz the biobeds in the first room, Captain Kirk signaled. *"McCoy, Kirk here. Will you and Dr. Luz please bring the vaccine and meet us in transporter room three."*

Dr. McCoy nodded. "On our way, Captain."

And just like that, Luz's bad mood was gone. They were going down to the station! She almost couldn't believe it.

Luz hurried after Dr. McCoy, struck by a pang of regret. She hadn't done much to further herself with her target. She had been helpful in replicating the vaccine, and she had been pleasant and pleasing in her ways. Yet her irritation at Tasm's dim-witted decisions had surely affected her characterization.

So Luz was determined to be ingratiating as they proceeded through concentric rings of long, curving corridors. She asked questions about the rooms she saw, and found out that each crew member had an enormous amount of space to themselves. Her glimpse of one of the quarters proved it was three times as big as the Petraw command booth on board their ship. Even that Andorian, who was spoiled with the best in goods and technology, hadn't had such an opulent allotment of personal space.

They returned to the transporter room where they had first arrived. Tasm and Kad were waiting with Captain Kirk. Tasm appeared exhilarated while Kad was covertly scanning the pattern buffers on the transporter.

Kirk's body language indicated he was suspicious, but he seemed to be conversing with Tasm in a more comfortable manner. Tasm was actually flirting with him in front of the transporter chief. "I'm sure my senior officers would be glad to attend a reception this evening to celebrate our alliance."

"What alliance?" McCoy asked.

Kirk kept a speculative gaze on Tasm. "We're going to work together to explore the station and get it operational before the Klingons arrive."

"More Klingons?" McCoy asked ironically. "Why am I not surprised?"

"We've got less than two days, Bones."

Luz noted Kirk's use of a nickname for McCoy. The

captain had done it earlier, too. Apparently these two officers were closer than Tasm had anticipated, or she would never have assigned Luz to McCoy. Tasm was biased against her just because Luz had disagreed with the way things were run during that fateful Andorian engagement. But Luz had been right. They had barely succeeded in getting the Andorian vessel—and it was due to her quick thinking and decisive action that they had taken it at all.

Kirk ordered, "You're with us, Doctor. We need to administer the vaccine to the landing party."

McCoy grimaced at being told he was returning to the station so soon.

"Kirk to bridge," Kirk said. "Drop the shield."

After a moment, a voice responded, *"Shield disengaged, sir."*

Luz could feel the tension from the Starfleet officers, who were almost expecting an attack. That wasn't good. Tasm should be lulling their suspicions, not confusing them into compliance.

Now that she considered it, Luz's initial elation faded. They weren't going to be able to do much inside the station with these Starfleet officers looking over their shoulders every step of the way.

"Sir," the transporter chief spoke up. "For some reason, our targeting sensors can't penetrate the shell of diburnium and osmium. I'll have to transport you into the entrance chamber. The upper part is rock."

Kirk acknowledged as Luz took her place on one of the pattern buffers. Kad was frowning slightly, obviously thinking the same thing—how long could they sustain their characters when they knew so little about the Kalandans? Why hadn't Tasm convinced the Starfleet officers to leave the station? But no, Tasm was smiling like she was glad they were coming along.

"Energize," Kirk ordered.

As the transporter dematerialized her, Luz was busy thinking of ways she could salvage something from this engagement. It looked like once again Tasm had taken on more than she could handle.

Mr. Spock was waiting with Mr. Sulu and Security Guard Reinhart in the entrance chamber. After he had rescued them from the sealed and airless chamber, they had immediately ceased their explorations of the Kalandan station, as per Captain Kirk's orders.

The landing party materialized, and Kirk introduced Commander Tasm and her officers. Spock noticed that McCoy stayed near the Kalandan medical technician and always seemed to be speaking to her. Luz made a pretense of helping as the doctor administered the vaccine to all three men.

Before beaming down, Kirk had briefly shared his misgivings with Spock about these newly arrived Kalandans. However, Spock believed it was logical to exhaust every opportunity for exploration. He was unable to form an opinion about the Kalandans until he could examine their behavior.

"Let's proceed to the command center," the captain suggested. "Sulu and Reinhart, you stay here."

Sulu murmured an acknowledgment. Neither of them were in top condition after their near-asphyxiation. But clearly Kirk didn't want to leave the entrance to the station unguarded while the shield was down.

Commander Tasm walked by Kirk's side down the corridor, with Spock directly behind. Officer Kad fell in next to Spock, behind his commander. Kad seemed interested in the botany labs, craning his neck to see inside, but Kirk didn't pause on the way through.

Bringing up the rear were the two doctors. "I've heard they used to terraform the surface on these old stations," Luz was saying to McCoy.

"You should see what the surface used to look like," McCoy replied. "Simply breathtaking!"

Spock dismissed the idle chatter as they passed through the oval nexus chamber.

Then Kirk gestured to the corridors that spread out around them. "Here're the living quarters we just discovered."

"These quarters must hold a wealth of information about our ancestors." Commander Tasm hesitated at one cross-corridor, as if wanting to go inside one of the rooms.

"Not as much as you would think," Kirk said gently. "Mostly like the object I gave you. A few personal belongings they packed up, I suppose after each one died."

Commander Tasm displayed a remarkable restraint of emotion. "The sporophyte virus kills slowly."

There was an awkward silence that Spock associated with a rather useless phenomenon known as survivor guilt. Naturally, he felt nothing. For a moment there was only the soft pad of their footsteps in the empty corridor.

Then Kirk ventured, in a deceptively mild tone, "In all these quarters, we've found no signs of children or their playthings. Is it common for your people to not bring children on their voyages?"

Commander Tasm looked speculative. "Are you

sure? Since we no longer maintain planetary stations such as these, it's difficult to know. Most Kalandans are concentrated in colonies, and there we have plenty of children. But there are no children on board my long-range ship."

Spock spoke up from behind. "This station was certainly created to be a long-range vessel."

"Do you have children living on the *Enterprise?*" Tasm asked.

"No," Kirk said. "It's felt that it's too dangerous on a ship that explores unknown territory."

"Is that what you think?"

Kirk hesitated. "I have enough people to take care of already."

Commander Tasm was nodding as they entered the command center. Spock noted that Kirk held back, waiting for the Kalandans to reveal what they knew about the station. Tasm first looked up at the computer node in the ceiling as the colors rippled across the surface.

Then she went straight to the command chair and sat down.

The Losira replica appeared, standing to face Tasm. Seeing them both together, the resemblance was less marked. The colored eyelids and brows were similar, but the underlying shape of Tasm's bone structure was different from Losira's. However, five hundred generations of mutations and interbreeding could cause that degree of change in a species.

"I am Commander Tasm, of the Kalandan Beta-nine colony. We detected your energy signal and we came to find you."

Losira looked closer. "You are different from the last one," she said in her lyrical voice.

"Didn't he introduce himself?" Tasm asked, glancing at Kirk.

"No."

Tasm smiled, making her resemblance to Losira more marked. "He didn't understand what a sophisticated replica you are."

Spock raised one brow and met Kirk's ironic shrug. Indeed.

Tasm explained to Losira, "That was Captain James T. Kirk of the Starfleet *Starship Enterprise*. You wouldn't know about the Federation, they're a new territorial entity."

"I also know of no Kalandan Beta-nine colony." The Losira replica seemed very interested, not as dreamy and detached as she had been with Kirk.

"Of course not," Tasm told her. "We are ten thousand years in your future. You are our ancestors, and we are the descendants of your children. We have been looking for this science station for hundreds of generations. But you've been lost to us."

Spock thought it was unusual for Commander Tasm to make an emotional appeal to a computer program. However, the Losira replica had consistently displayed emotional responses, so perhaps it was the correct course of action.

Right now the Losira replica was looking slightly stricken. But as Spock had observed, she was not programmed to ask questions, only to give information.

Tasm raised both her hands, palm up. "We need your help to make this station operational. While the Starfleet officers were stranded on the station, they damaged the defense computer. We must fix it before other ships arrive and try to take possession of the station by force."

"The defense computer is currently malfunctioning," Losira agreed. But nothing happened.

Kirk was looking determined, as he always did when confronted with the Losira replica. He almost spoke, but Tasm was focused, her fingers tightly gripping the armrest. Spock noted she only had four fingers instead of five, like Losira.

"There must be a way," Tasm urged. "Show us how to get to the defense computer so we can fix it."

Losira gestured. Abruptly a door appeared in the wall of the command center. "This corridor will take you to the defense computer."

McCoy let out a strangled cry, pointing to the door, while the Kalandan doctor looked stunned. Even Kirk was surprised. "All I had to do was ask!" he murmured to Spock.

"So it appears." Spock considered it to be logical. Every door in the station had opened when presented with the correct few words.

Tasm beamed at the Losira replica. "We'll get to work and keep you apprised."

Kirk joined Commander Tasm as she approached the doorway, refusing to relinquish the lead to Officer Kad. McCoy hung back to say to Spock, "So it looks like they really *are* Kalandans."

"That remains to be seen," Spock replied noncommittally. "However, the fact that you still doubt is apparent."

"No, not at all. I feel that we should trust them. Luz is a fine technician—"

"I cannot assist you with your feelings, Doctor."

McCoy threw up his hands. "Doesn't anything ever get you excited, Mr. Spock?"

Spock unslung his tricorder and prepared the sensors to search and record. "I fail to see what my level of excitement has to do with adequately performing my duty."

Spock stepped into the corridor to follow the captain and the Kalandans. Emotions would merely interfere with his work. He preferred to take tricorder readings of everything he encountered and properly analyze those.

Spock ignored McCoy's muttering through the entire length of the long sloping corridor until they entered another oval chamber. This was the first large-scale space they had found inside the station. The ceiling was twice as high as the chambers on the upper levels.

Another square computer node was mounted in the center overhead. Directly underneath it was a square casing four point two meters wide and three point nine-six meters high. It had slots and screens on the two sides Spock could observe, with small black windows set into the smooth white surface. The computer node overhead was muted, with the colors hardly moving, similar to the cube in the entrance chamber.

Spock examined the readout on his tricorder. "The computer node is inert, Captain. There is currently minimal power levels being emitted by the computer bank below."

"So this is the defense computer," Kirk said slowly.

Spock circled the computer bank to see the other panels. Kirk was next to him. Both stopped short when they saw the archway behind the computer bank.

It was a freestanding arch. The shape was nearly square, with thick legs and a lintel that crossed over their heads. Though the computer bank and the rest of the room were made of the usual bright white osmium, the arch was constructed of burnished blue neutronium. The base of each leg was molded in a series of bulging and incised shapes. An etched design ran across the top lintel, which Spock carefully recorded. After running a comparison, it didn't conform to any pattern of elements found in the Starfleet database.

"What is it, Spock?" Kirk asked as the Kalandans approached the arch.

"Unknown, Captain." Spock quickly analyzed his tricorder readings. "Primarily neutronium in construction. My tricorder is unable to penetrate the surface."

"Is it part of the computer?"

"Perhaps, Captain. Consider this device." Spock aimed his tricorder at a cylindrical unit attached to the outside of the computer bank. Like the arch, its outer casing was made of burnished blue neutronium. Spock could read numerous internal components inside the computer bank. None included elemental neutronium.

"Do you know what this is?" Kirk asked Commander Tasm.

Her wonder and excitement were clear in her expression. It was the first time Spock had observed an excess of emotion from the Kalandan. "I've never seen anything like this before."

Tasm put her hand on the cylindrical unit. It was ten point two centimeters in diameter and forty-eight point six-five centimeters long. Her two officers seemed similarly baffled.

Kirk glanced up at the muted node in the ceiling. "Was it damaged by our phasers?"

"I will endeavor to ascertain that, Captain."

Wasting no time, Spock immediately began his preliminary examination. First Officer Kad also circled the computer bank, touching various parts of an unusual padd that folded out from a pocket-sized unit to a micro-thin screen.

Kad nodded slightly in an acknowledgment, which Spock returned. The Kalandan was admirably self-restrained, confining himself to comments about the work at hand.

It appeared they would be cooperating fully with the Kalandans in their investigation of the defense computer. Spock approved. In his opinion, scientists were natural allies. It often took a joint effort to fully comprehend the unknown.

Chapter Eleven

TASM DIDN'T WASTE TIME congratulating herself on getting access to the defense computer. It wasn't difficult to manipulate computer programs, since by design they were predictable. Captain Kirk's reports had stated that the computer logarithms retained Losira's emotional response. Since Commander Losira had left the station on defense mode to await the return of Kalandans, that's what Tasm had given her: Kalandan descendants in trouble. Kirk had assisted in crafting her appeal by giving her insight into why the Kalandans didn't have children on board. With so much rich material to work with, it was easy to convince the Losira replica to help her.

Now they had access to the defense computer, and it looked promising. According to Kad's preliminary report submitted through the feed in their padds, the neutronium device might, in fact, be capable of dimensional transport across interstellar distances. Of minor importance; Kad had also discovered advances in micro-monofilament relays and conversion infusers.

144

Tasm took the opportunity when Dr. McCoy returned to the *Enterprise* to send Luz back to their ship. Then she ordered Marl down to the Kalandan station. His target was the chief engineer on board the *Enterprise,* and Tasm wanted to give him the edge he would need with this unique technology.

Captain Kirk also made changes in personnel, bringing down two new security guards to replace the officers who had been stranded inside the station with him. Tasm almost disputed his assumption that Starfleet would maintain security over the station, but decided it was a moot point at this juncture.

Kirk himself didn't return to the ship. Instead, he frowned thoughtfully as he replaced his communicator. "I wonder what else Losira will tell us now that you're here."

Tasm accompanied Kirk back to the command center. She regretted having to leave the defense computer, but anything Kirk learned about the Kalandans, she would need to know as well. Both of her pod-mates were quite capable of examining the defense computer, so she gracefully gave in to the demands of her character.

Kirk seated himself in the command chair and Losira appeared. "Greetings Captain James T. Kirk of the Starfleet *Starship Enterprise,*" Losira stated.

"Yes . . ." Kirk hesitated. "I'm sorry I didn't introduce myself earlier. I didn't understand that it was . . . necessary."

Tasm suppressed her amused reaction at Kirk's obvious attraction to the holographic program. Whatever was important to him was important to her character. That was the way to get what the Petraw needed.

"We've located the defense computer and are attempting to repair it now," Kirk was telling Losira. "But we need to have access to the station's engines. We need navigational power before the Klingons arrive."

Losira's smile was wistful. "That information is controlled by the defense computer."

"The defense computer is under repair."

Losira merely waited for a request or question.

"Can't you show us the engines, so we can protect this station?" Kirk asked.

"That information is controlled by the defense computer."

Kirk stood up. "You ask her."

Tasm sat down in the offered seat. "Losira has already given you the answer. She will likely defer requests for further access to the station to the defense computer."

Kirk folded his arms. "Your people certainly are cautious, Commander."

Tasm again shrugged. "How else does a civilization survive for tens of thousands of years? But there is one thing I do want to know." Tasm turned to Losira. "Why didn't you use the dimensional transporter to get help from your home star when your crew became infected with the virus?"

The Losira replica looked downcast. "Our fellow Kalandans closed the portals in the colonies to prevent contamination from spreading. We have maintained our isolation and have refrained from using our portal to reach any other location. We await the supply ships that will bring relief to my people."

Tasm seemed satisfied. "The virus must have crossed

back to our people through the portal. That's what started the initial plagues."

"I see," Kirk said noncommittally.

Tasm continued with a series of questions: "How long were the scientists stationed on the planetoid?" "What was the mission of the advance force?" "How many worlds did the scientists come from?" "How big was Kalandan territory in your time?"

Most of her questions were referred to the defense computer.

"Have you recorded Losira's logs?" Tasm asked Kirk. She already knew the answer, well aware that Kirk had not mentioned the existence of the logs yet.

Kirk seemed discomforted. "Most of them, yes. Then we discovered the living quarters and began searching in there."

"May we copy your record of the logs?" Tasm requested. "That way, my crew can examine them against our database."

Kirk agreed. She sensed his reluctance as he gave the order to his crew for the data transfer from their computer to her ship.

Tasm held her slight smile, remaining composed. She had been working toward that request since they had accessed the station. Now she would know everything that Kirk knew about the Kalandans.

It was always good to make the target feel as if they were getting something extra.

Tasm stood up, facing Kirk. Moving closer, she tilted her head back. Though they stood eye-to-eye, it gave the illusion that she was smaller, more defenseless than him. Sex roles were critical and surprisingly complex in human culture. Tasm had spent extra time in the information feed, gaining expertise on the subject. She intended to obtain additional information for the Petraw database.

"Don't you find this exhilarating?" Her face was inside the range of intimate space.

Kirk stood very still. "Naturally, we don't have the personal connection to the station that you do."

Tasm drew in her breath, turning from him. She strolled away, tracing her hand on the chair. The memory of how Losira gestured and moved helped her stay in character. "It's been a pleasure working with you, Captain Kirk. I will be sure to praise you to my fellow Kalandans."

His eyes narrowed slightly as she started toward him, adding, "I want to give you something to show you my appreciation."

She went right up to him, standing so she almost touched him. His breath warmed the air. Her hand reached into her pocket, pulling out the small carved stone he had found inside the station.

She lifted it up between them. "Accept this historic artifact as the most meager token of my gratitude. I'm sure my people will do far more for you if given the chance. If you hadn't explored this station, the signal wouldn't have been sent. We owe you a debt of gratitude that can never be repaid. I can think of no other way to show you how deeply you have affected my people, except—"

Tasm broke off, leaning ever closer. Lightly she put her hand with the stone against his chest. She only had to reach out to touch her lips to his.

He shifted closer, his mouth responding, deepening the kiss. She tightened her fingers into his uniform.

Without warning, Kirk broke off contact. Both his hands were on her shoulders, gently pushing her away. There was an expression on his face—not quite doubtful, but uncomfortable. "I think that's more gratitude than I deserve."

Tasm acquiesced with a slight smile, but she pressed the stone into his hand anyway. He automatically took it, closing his fist around the artifact.

She thought it was an adequate start. "Let's get back to work."

For some human reason, Captain Kirk expected Tasm and some of her crew to join his senior officers at a "reception" on board the *Enterprise*. It was necessary that they further ingratiate themselves with the Starfleet officers, so Tasm agreed.

She returned to her ship before the reception to distribute the computer analysis of the Kalandan logs through the information feed to her pod-mates. After absorbing the information feed, Tasm would choose who to take to the reception with her. Kad and Marl would not be fully briefed, since they were only able to scan the analysis on their padds. But their attempt to repair the damaged defense computer was more important than cultural references.

It was customary for Tasm to stay resolutely in character even on board their scout ship. She wouldn't allow her "Losira" expression to slacken until she lay down in her cell to absorb the feed and meditate prior to their next encounter. Then she finally relaxed her muscles, allowing herself to consider the ramifications of acquiring interstellar transport technology.

It would revolutionize the Petraw civilization! Her

people were spread so far apart that it took generations for technology to make its way from one birthing world to the next. Using an interstellar portal, technological innovations could immediately be provided to every Petraw in the territory. Communication would also be instantaneous, rather than the slow relay of acquired data via their birthing world through the feed.

Lying snug in her cell, Tasm was almost breathless with the possibilities. This was one technological find that wouldn't be sent back on an automated drone. They would take the portal to Petraw territory themselves, protecting it along the way.

She knew she was now leading a priority engagement, the first their scout ship had encountered. She was determined to succeed. Closing her eyes, she began to meditate on the Kalandan analysis in the information feed.

If not for the refreshing idea that Luz would be at the reception, McCoy would have been irritated about squeezing into a dress uniform and engaging in small talk. He had spent days working like a fiend to find a cure for the virus, with his only break a few hours' sleep on the hard ground. Under the circumstances, he would have thought it impossible to be charming in such a tight collar.

But that Kalandan doctor was something special. That's how he found himself standing next to Luz in the observation lounge, trying not to dribble synthehol down the front of his blue satin uniform.

Everything looked festive. There were eight or nine senior officers present. Neither Spock nor Scotty were there—not that Spock ever enlivened a social occasion.

They were both down on the station, working on the Kalandan defense computer.

McCoy had his own opinions about repairing the defense computer. He thought they should leave it alone. They had lost three men before disabling it the last time. And after treating Sulu and Reinhart for the damage done by oxygen deprivation, McCoy was also not too keen on sending so many people down to the station to search the living quarters. Six teams in all, with one Kalandan and one Starfleet officer on each.

While the methodical cataloging continued on the station, the reception was in full swing. Uhura and Chekov were talking to Commander Tasm and Captain Kirk in the back of the lounge. Dr. M'Benga was chatting with another female Kalandan officer called Mlan. She had dramatic black hair and brows like the Kalandan commander. Sulu was sampling the typically eclectic Federation spread along with a seemingly young crewman, Officer Pir. Pir was a relatively plump Kalandan who seemed nervous in spite of, or perhaps because of, his constant smile.

All four of the Kalandans dressed exactly the same, with dark coveralls closed to the base of their necks. They obviously didn't believe in evening wear. Other than the arrangement of their hair, it was tough to tell them apart. But Luz's blue-green eyelids were distinctive. Then again, that might be because he had a special regard for her.

He spent as much time with Luz as he could. She kept closing her eyes and swaying to the jazz playing in the background, undoubtedly summoned up by the captain's yeoman. McCoy appreciated the sight of her enjoyment.

The yeoman's tasteful touches could also be seen in the fresh-cut flowers on the table, and the dim lighting that emphasized the starry vista beyond the observation wall. The curve of the planetoid loomed in the lower corner of the window. Its appearance was deceptive: it looked like a typical Class-M planet with blue water and brown land masses. Spock had discovered that this illusion was also created by the magnetic inversion. Undoubtedly the station was designed to masquerade as a natural planet, orbiting in a solar system while the Kalandans covertly performed their investigations.

Slightly above the *Enterprise* was the red Kalandan ship with its odd bulging hull.

"This is going to sound strange," McCoy told Luz. "But I don't know the name of your ship."

Luz gestured dismissal. "It doesn't have a name."

"Surely it must have some designation," McCoy insisted.

Luz hesitated. "It's scout ship *Y8847.* I'm sure that's meaningless to you."

McCoy found himself nodding acceptance, but it *was* unusual. Most alien species gave names to their vessels. And according to Scotty's report, the Kalandan ship had seen a lot of light-years, with certain pitting in the hull that could only be caused by uninterrupted decades in space.

"Do you prefer to be on the ship rather than the colony?" McCoy asked.

Luz seemed uncomfortable, and actually glanced around before answering, "Frankly, I'd really rather be on our planet. All this space travel is not what I had hoped for when I was growing up."

McCoy thought she was refreshing. He sometimes

felt like he was surrounded by space-mad youngsters who were unduly eager to be roaming around the galaxy. They had no idea how dangerous it was.

Luz reached out and squeezed his arm sympathetically. "I can tell you'd rather be resting in your own quarters."

"A delightful thought," McCoy admitted, knowing she wouldn't take offense.

Luz glanced at the mostly empty trays of food. "The reception appears to be almost over. You'll be done with work soon."

Regretfully McCoy shook his head. "I'm not finished for the night. I have something to do in sickbay."

"Oh? What is that?"

"We've delayed bringing up D'Amato's body. D'Amato was in the landing party with us, but he was killed by the defense computer our first day on the station." McCoy felt his throat tighten.

"Why do you need to bring his body to the ship?" Luz asked.

"So we can place it in stasis until it can be returned to his family."

"Returned . . ." Luz said with a faintly horrified expression.

"Yes, for burial." Since she still seemed confused, McCoy asked, "What do you do with your people who die?"

"The body is disintegrated. It's of no use once they're dead."

"Luz!" Commander Tasm was standing right behind him. McCoy hadn't heard her approach. "Come, we are departing."

"So soon?" McCoy automatically asked.

Tasm stared at Luz as if silently commanding her to move. Luz seemed flustered, joining the other Kalandans after bidding McCoy a hurried good night.

Chekov volunteered to escort the Kalandans to the transporter room. As they left, Kirk sauntered over to McCoy.

McCoy lifted his glass in a toast. "Well, that was a success."

Kirk's brow furrowed. "Something's not right."

"What's wrong? I thought everything was going fine."

"I don't trust them, Bones." Kirk seemed preoccupied.

"What's not to trust? They saved the ship, they gave us the vaccine, then they found the defense computer for us. What more do you want?"

"I don't know." Kirk was staring after the Kalandans.

McCoy drained the last of his drink. "Well, if you want to spend your time worrying about people who've done nothing but help us, you can, but I've got better things to do. Like getting reacquainted with my own bed."

Kirk grimaced, and McCoy was sorry he'd been so blunt. But what else could he say? He clapped a reassuring hand on the captain's shoulder before he left for sickbay. It was best not to mention to Kirk that he was going to disinter D'Amato's body for removal to Earth. No wonder Jim was so edgy. He had a lot on his mind.

Luz knew that Tasm was incensed by the way her nostrils flared with every breath. But Tasm restrained herself as they made their way to the transporter room.

It was different when they materialized back on their

scout ship. As soon as the lowering walls closed around them, Tasm exclaimed, "Are you defective? You spoke about a taboo with your target."

Luz couldn't think of anything she'd said wrong. In fact, she was making more progress with her target than any of the others were. Dr. McCoy would do almost anything she asked right now and not even think twice about it. But Pir had been hopeless at the reception, unable to maintain a simple conversation with anyone. That silly smile hadn't helped.

Mlan and Pir stood awkwardly in the small space. But since Tasm hadn't dismissed them, they stayed to witness.

"Death," Tasm said flatly.

For a moment, Luz thought Tasm was ordering her to be put away. It had always been her fear, that her pod-mates would decide she was defective and summarily reject her. A hasty disintegration in the surgical unit, and she would cease to exist.

"No, Tasm!" Luz blurted out. "Not that!"

Tasm turned to Pir and Mlan. "She told her target that we disintegrate our dead."

Her pod-mates were taken aback, their eyes accusing. "Luz!" Pir blurted out. "You know death is one of the taboos."

"Didn't you meditate on the analysis of the Kalandan logs?" Tasm asked.

Luz hesitated. They had been ordered to their cells prior to the reception to absorb the information feed containing the computer analysis of the Kalandan logs. But Luz had never assumed a meditative state. She had been busy thinking about the glory their pod would receive when they returned with interstellar transport technology. A select few might even be brought into the birthing chamber, as they deserved.

But it would take the rest of her life to return to their birthing world, and anything could happen along on the way. It would be best for them to appropriate the Kalandan station and use it as a base so they could operate the portal while en route.

Luz had been so busy worrying over whether Tasm could bring them through this engagement successfully that she hadn't paid any attention to the information feed.

"There wasn't much time to absorb everything," she offered by way of excuse.

Tasm turned to Pir. "Tell me, what did the logs say the Kalandans do with the scientists who died."

Pir obediently recited, "The Kalandan dead are stored in cryogenic chambers."

"The Kalandans used their dead for science experiments," Tasm said. "Yet you just told your target that the body is useless once it's dead."

"Ten thousand years have supposedly passed," Luz quickly pleaded. "Things can be different now."

Tasm was impassive. "You violated a taboo and deviated from the common character line, Luz."

Pir and Mlan were looking even more reproachful. Luz knew she had made a mistake. Was the surgical unit next?

"You need me," Luz insisted. "I'm making real progress with the doctor. Next time I'll meditate harder on the feed. I'll do better . . ."

"Go to your cell," Tasm ordered.

Luz felt an immense relief that she wasn't being taken to the surgical unit. It was instantly followed by a stab of resentment. It wasn't *that* critical a mistake. Even Tasm had made mistakes on this engagement.

Luz knew she was being singled out because she didn't always agree with the others. And Tasm was waiting for her to make a mistake, any mistake, so she could be disciplined. Look at Pir and Mlan—those mindless automatons were following Luz to the cells. The Petraw might as well send out androids instead of scouts.

Luz dragged her feet the closer she and Tasm got to the cells.

"Get in there and meditate on the feed," Tasm ordered.

Luz took a deep breath. "All I need is another repeat."

Tasm waited impassively for her to slip inside. Luz could see the conviction in her hard eyes. If she didn't get inside the cell, she might get dragged to the surgical unit. Pir and Mlan would do it, too. They would do whatever Tasm told them to do, because she was the leader of this engagement.

Luz ducked her head and crawled into the cell. She had no other choice. She was doomed to wander the stars in a life constrained by her narrow pod-mates.

Tasm sealed the cell on Luz. She could see Luz's fist beating on the semi-transparent seal. Some Petraw needed more instruction than others. Another four hundred crons of the information feed on a continuous loop should be more than enough. Luz would have to meditate sometime, and then the information would be part of her memory.

Tasm wasn't about to risk their cover. If Luz continued to be uncooperative when she came out of the cell, Tasm was prepared to detach her permanently from this engagement. At this point it would be difficult to explain her absence to Dr. McCoy, but he was apparently a minor target anyway. Tasm was prepared to take any measures necessary to ensure the success of this mission.

Chapter Twelve

SPOCK WORKED right through the evening with Kad, the Kalandan second officer. Thus far, Kad had only smiled once, when his commander had opened the doorway to the defense computer. After that, he was civil enough, but he concentrated on the work at hand.

Spock preferred him to Officer Marl, the Kaladan engineer. Marl was a tall man who shuffled when he walked. His head was slightly bowed, a subconscious sign of deference that was unnecessary. They appeared to be standard humanoids, though thinner than average. Their most outstanding feature was their multicolored eyelids. Kad had yellow and brown streaks, while Marl had red and purple layers.

Marl had evidently taken a liking to Mr. Scott, remaining by the engineer's side after Scott transported down. Warp capability had been restored on the *Enterprise,* and Scotty had managed to whisper to Spock, "She's nearly set back t' rights! Shields are up t' eighty-seven percent!"

Spock didn't indulge in useless praise. The engineer had merely done his duty. He assigned Scott and Marl to assess the damage to the monofilaments leading from the processor to what appeared to be an energy source. They had already cut off sections of the outer casing of plasticized osmium, revealing the interior of the computer core. The modules of the nanoprocessor units were sealed and set in rows of ten, numbering nearly one thousand in all. The modules were linked together by bundles of monofilaments.

Scott and Marl were working in the base of the computer, under the processor, attempting to examine the power supply. From the grunts and muttered words that were exchanged, it appeared that some progress was being made.

Sifting through the monofilaments, Spock tested each one with a laser wand. Many were sealed inside from the phaser damage. Security Guard Reinhart's phaser had been on setting four, producing a thermal shock wave that had been carried through the monofilaments to the defense computer bank. The effects of the thermal radiation had leaped the incoming bundles of monofilaments, and had sealed many of the links between the modules as well.

"Do your people still employ monofilaments as data and energy carriers?" Spock inquired.

"No, our forcefield conduits are more efficient." Kad glanced up. "If it's true that your ship was dimensionally transported nine hundred and ninety point seven light-years away, perhaps the monofilaments control the flux in the excessive amount of power needed."

Spock looked at Kad with interest. "That would be a

logical method of regulating the power from a magnetic field generator."

Kad was also examining the slagged monofilaments. "What sort of distribution system do your people use?"

"The *Enterprise* employs a network of optical monocrystal microfibers to relay data. Much of our power distribution is through a series of high-energy waveguide conduits."

"Your optical microfibers might be compatible with this system," Kad suggested thoughtfully.

"Perhaps," Spock conceded. "We would need to examine the interior of a module to determine the method of connection. What memory storage medium was used by your ancestors?"

"We know so little about that time." Kad shook his head. "Now we use a series of stasis fields to increase the processing rate. But these modules are too small, and there's no plasma manifolds to control the stasis field. Should we begin taking apart a module?"

"First the integrity of the system must be verified," Spock decided.

Spock used the laser wand to randomly test approximately one-fifth of the monofilaments. It took hours, resulting in only one conclusion. "The integrity of this system has been irreversibly compromised. Seventy-six percent of the monofilaments on the exterior port connection have been sealed by the phaser discharge."

Scotty popped out from under the processor in time to hear. "Well, she's got access to power. Th' bundles of monofilaments feed through this level and pass a stasis field our instruments canna penetrate. But th' monofilaments are clear an' functioning! None show signs of any damage."

Kad was working on the lower modules. "It appears the thermal discharge wave hit the computer and was slowed down by the data storage modules. Twenty-seven percent of the monofilaments down here are damaged."

Scotty smacked the side of the computer bank with one hand. "She's scrap," Scotty said bluntly. "Ye'll be getting nothing out of this computer."

Marl's head was hanging as if it was his fault.

"I believe you are correct, Mr. Scott," Spock agreed.

With that, Scotty stretched to his fullest height, raising his hands as high as they would go. "That's it fer me then! I'm getting some shut-eye."

"Very well, Mr. Scott. Please inform the captain that my own report will be ready for him shortly."

"You're not going to stay, Mr. Spock!" Scotty's voice lowered and he moved closer to Spock. "You've been up for two days, man."

"I will meditate later," Spock evenly replied. "Good night, Mr. Scott."

Scott threw up his hands, as though he thought Spock was acting irrationally, but he didn't try to convince him to retire.

Marl looked disappointed, but he just watched Mr. Scott leave the chamber. "What about directly accessing the data modules using another processor?"

"That is one possibility." Spock slowly circled the exposed computer bank. "However, we have limited time and must target our goal."

Both Kalandans nodded as though they understood that reasoning.

With the excessive number of monofilament links destroyed, it was not likely that the data in the modules could be accessed in a coherent fashion. Computer modules were notoriously difficult to crack. Some were contained with extremely low pressure to aid in faster-than-light calculations. Radiation or powerful magnetic fields were often employed.

"In my opinion," Spock told them, "the danger of opening a module far exceeds the knowledge to be gained at this point."

He circled the computer to the arch. Not far away, the cylinder made of neutronium was attached to the side of the computer bank. "However, this device is unique. The cylinder and the archway appear to be a unit. They may form the subspace matrix through which matter can be dimensionally transported."

The cylindrical unit appeared to be joined to the bottom layer of nanoprocessor modules through a bundle of monofilaments. Spock tested several dozen and found none had been damaged.

The bundles of monofilaments fed through a single access port on the side of the cylindrical unit. Kad saw what Spock was doing, and he traced one bundle down the side of the computer. He had to go underneath the processor to see where the monofilaments emerged. "This bundle disappears into a port in the flooring," his muffled voice said.

There was no access panel, so it took some work to cut the plasticized osmium flooring. Marl proved to be adept with the maser-saw. He also did much of the heavy lifting, prying up balky sections of floor with brute force. Spock offered assistance, knowing his superior strength would make quick work of the job, but Marl appeared to gain a great deal of enjoyment from the task and carried on.

With several sections of the flooring up, Kad noted, "These bundles are going to the arch." Marl's reaction was much noisier and enthusiastic. He cut into larger swaths of flooring to reveal the entire length of the monofilament conduit. It led directly from the cylindrical unit to the nearby arch.

Kad was serious. "Can we make the portal work without the computer?"

"Unknown." Spock aimed his tricorder at the arch. "My tricorder is unable to penetrate the stasis collar around the port."

"We have a microfocus sensor that may work." Kad searched in the case their ship had beamed down. Spock had seen various useful tools come out of it.

Marl handed Kad a slender sensor unit with a pointed tip. "I tried it on the port leading to the energy source, but the magnetic flux scrambled the signal."

Kad gripped the sensor and knelt down next to the base of the arch. "This port isn't leading to any energy source. It may be able to tell us what's behind the neutronium casing."

The unit beeped and flashed a series of lights. After a few moments, Kad stood up and pressed the sensor into a slightly larger diagnostic unit. He showed Spock the screen, which had a readout of the percentages of elements present, a mass analysis, and a scrolling schematic of the exact location of the molecular distribution.

Kad explained what they were seeing. "The monofilaments enter the port, then appear to be melded with the neutronium core of the arch. There's only a small volume of empty space; the rest of the arch must be solid neutronium."

"Fascinating." Spock briefly considered whether a fusion technique had been used to create such a large structure of neutronium. It was beyond the current capabilities of Starfleet scientists.

Kad merely shrugged, but Marl looked disappointed. "Let's try the cylinder. It can't be solid neutronium, too."

Spock moved away from the computer bank so Kad could place the pointed end of the sensor against the port where the monofilament bundles emerged. The unit beeped and flashed thirty-four point two seconds longer than the first time.

Kad showed Spock the diagnostic unit. "The monofilaments are attached to eighteen junction nodes. It doesn't appear that monofilament linkages are used inside the unit itself. The junction nodes themselves are in cryostatic suspension."

Spock raised one brow. "Indeed? That would indicate that cytoplasmic relays are used."

"The inside of this unit is nothing like the rest of this computer system," Kad agreed. "Most of the components joined by the junction nodes are encased in neutronium, impenetrable to this sensor."

Spock considered the information they had gathered thus far. "The computer bank is one unit, while the cylinder and archway are another. It appears to be a melding of disparate technological elements, much like the construction of your ship."

Kad looked faintly startled, while Marl actually laughed out loud. "I guess that's one thing that hasn't changed about my people. We're open to updating our systems if something better comes along."

Spock ascertained that the third and largest bundle of

monofilaments from the cylindrical unit penetrated the same port that appeared to provide energy to the computer bank. He borrowed Kad's microfocus sensor and diagnostic unit to check these monofilaments. They appeared to be fully charged.

"The cylinder and archway are connected directly to the power source," Spock announced. "However, the Losira replica indicated that full power would not be authorized except by the defense computer."

"This computer isn't authorizing anything," Marl pointed out.

"It can't be repaired," Kad agreed. "So that means we can't operate the interstellar portal."

"Unless . . ." Spock considered the design of the computer processor. "Thus far, every system on this station has operated on an as-needed basis. Since full power can be authorized by this computer, the magnetic generator may simply comply if power is called for from this location."

"Then we might be able to get the portal functional!" Marl kicked aside some of the sections of flooring he had just removed. He was clearly impatient to get to work. "Let's do it."

Spock opened his communicator. *"Enterprise,* Spock here. Please replicate a transporter self-diagnostic subprocessor with its own power source."

From the ship, the third-watch communications officer acknowledged, *"Aye, sir. I'll have the replicator unit get to work on it right away."*

Spock acknowledged and signed off. Then he explained to the Kalandans, "We shall test your theory that our monocrystal microfibers are compatible with the monofilaments. I will attempt to bypass the original computer using a new subprocessor. A high-level, self-diagnostic program may be able to determine what commands are required."

"That sounds reasonable." Kad began scanning the cube in the ceiling. "What about these computer nodes? Can we reactivate them if we get the portal operational?"

"My examination of the node in the entrance chamber indicated it was damaged beyond repair. The tricorder readings of the node in this chamber are identical."

"Then we've lost the directional units," Kad said.

Spock calmly pointed out, "The fact that the nodes are not functional lessens the potential for the portal to be used as a weapon, as it was in our case."

Kad looked determined, while Marl wasn't as enthused any longer. "We must report to our commander about this."

Spock agreed and made arrangements to meet them back in the portal chamber when the subprocessor had been replicated. The Kalandans said they would need to meditate for a short time, as Spock intended to do.

Before they left, Spock tried to return the microfocus sensor and diagnostic unit. But Kad refused, shutting their case and sealing it. "We have plenty on the ship. You may need it again."

Spock hesitated, though it appeared perfectly harmless. Perhaps he was influenced by the captain's lingering distrust of the Kalandans. Yet he pocketed the handheld sensor device, to take it up to the *Enterprise* so he could examine it. It could indeed be a useful device during the work ahead.

* * *

Captain Kirk had only been stuck in the Kalandan station for a few days, but it felt strange to be back in his quarters on board the *Enterprise*. Despite the several glasses of synthehol that he'd had at the reception, he couldn't make himself lie down to sleep. He trusted his alert feeling. They were in danger.

Kirk read through Spock's latest report, filed before the Vulcan retired for a bit of reviving meditation. So it appeared they had indeed located the interstellar transporter. Spock hoped to be able to get it functioning again.

Kirk got dressed in his duty uniform. He could feel the pressure of unknown vessels descending on them—the Klingons and every other scavenger out there who had intercepted that strong energy burst from the interstellar portal. The Klingons would be out for blood, since their Defense Force cruiser had been destroyed.

And he didn't trust these Kalandans. . . .

It was that kiss. He had realized it during the reception when Tasm had flirtatiously brushed against his arm, then let her gaze focus on his mouth. She was trying to seduce him, and it might have worked, except for that kiss.

It was an experience unlike any other. He had been the object of seduction before. Eve McHuron, Harry Mudd's associate, had not needed a Venus drug to make her kiss seductive. Elaan of Troyius had been petulantly provocative, trying to manipulate him, yet underneath she was just a scared young woman. On the other hand, Lenore, daughter of Kodos the Executioner, had been insane. Yet he hadn't guessed it from her warm and loving embrace.

Kissing Tasm made him feel like he was under a microscope. He had felt weirdly removed from the experience.

Even more unpleasant, the image of Captain Mox flashed through his mind as her lips touched his. All of those Klingons, killed without a second thought. Tasm had never mentioned regret over what she had done.

McCoy kept insisting that the Kalandans were helping them. It was true that it should be enough, but Kirk questioned why Tasm had given them no new information about the Kalandans. The exchange of cultural and legal information, as proscribed by Starfleet's diplomatic protocols, had been skimpy on the Kalandan side.

After spending a whole day with Tasm, Kirk still didn't know her very well. She didn't talk much about herself—her needs or desires. Her responses to his questions were almost cloying, as if she was humoring him. Also she was not as attractive as he had originally thought.

But she got what she wanted almost every time. Kirk wasn't sure why he had agreed to send down only a few search teams, when he wanted to comb the station with every available hand. She resisted because she didn't want Starfleet occupying the station in greater numbers. She had finally, and reluctantly it seemed, told him the size of her crew. It was surprisingly small for the size of her ship.

Kirk frowned as he glanced around his quarters. Now that he was back on board the *Enterprise,* he wanted nothing more than to be inside the Kalandan station.

He attached a communicator to his belt and grabbed a tricorder. "Bridge, Kirk here. I'm transporting down to the station. Alert me if anyone from the Kalandan ship beams down as well."

The two Starfleet security guards in the entrance chamber said that only the search teams were currently inside the station. Spock and the Kalandan officers were scheduled to be transporting back down shortly, to begin installing the new computer.

Kirk didn't linger on the first level where ship's sensors could read his presence. Tasm had insisted that they would question Losira only when they were together. He had agreed, but that bothered him, too. What was Tasm worried about?

Going down the corridor, he avoided the search teams in the botany labs, alerted by their voices as they catalogued things left behind in the cupboards.

Voices also echoed down the long corridors of the living quarters. Sounds were oddly distorted by the muffling walls. He moved quickly across the corridors. Now that he was down a few levels, the forcefield layers would baffle the sensors.

In the command center, Kirk once again took the chair. Losira winked into existence. "Captain James T. Kirk," she said in greeting.

"Commander Losira," Kirk replied cordially.

He would be breaking what amounted to a diplomatic agreement if he questioned Losira alone. But he made his decision after one look at the Losira replica. Then he knew why he needed to see her again.

Kirk kept thinking that it couldn't be true, that Tasm couldn't be a descendent of Losira, because there was none of the cultural and physical refinement he expected to see in a developing civilization. He thought

Tasm and her officers were blunted in both intellectual response and individuality. For one thing, Tasm seemed completely unaware of her body, while every move Losira made was the embodiment of harmonious grace.

It was a gut feeling he had, and it came from knowledge of his own ancestors ten thousand years ago. Humans had just started creating agricultural civilizations, having been hunters and gatherers for hundreds of thousands of years. It was literally the stone age, with no real metallurgy. Yet he kept thinking there would be a stronger resemblance and sense of progression between him and that stone-age man than he could see between Tasm and Losira.

"The Kalandans seem like a highly developed civilization," Kirk said thoughtfully. "How far back does your history go?"

Losira seemed pleased she could answer his question. "Our people became space-faring in cycle 903."

"I don't know what a cycle is," Kirk told her. Thinking of a way to translate time, he suggested, "Show me a star map of that time."

Losira briefly closed her eyes. When she opened them, a sphere appeared and floated near her head. It looked as if it contained every shining star in their double-spiral galaxy. Kirk aimed his tricorder at the sphere to record it, then initiated a comparison analysis. The image was of the galaxy two hundred thousand years ago.

"That's impossible." Kirk didn't want to think of what humans had been like two hundred thousand years ago. "There must be some mistake."

"The Kalandans are an ancient civilization."

Kirk wasn't sure what to say. Suddenly his Earth-centric focus seemed a little absurd.

Losira's voice was dreamy. "We are descended from noble scientists who refused to serve their great and terrible people."

"What people?"

"That information is controlled by the defense computer."

Kirk shook his head. "Why am I not surprised?" He tried another tact. "Why did the Kalandans leave their people?"

"Our people were feared by the still-developing races throughout the region. The Kalandan scientists believed that the hostile attitudes of our people were wrong and would lead to the downfall of our civilization. They were proven correct. Not long after the Kalandan scientists left, the rest of our people were utterly destroyed."

Kirk nodded. "I've wondered myself at your ruthlessness. You can send a replica to kill with a touch, yet you're aware that it's wrong."

Losira looked pensive. "We are life-loving explorers, yet my people have a history of creating extremely destructive weapons."

Kirk knew his doubts were shaken. Losira was the end product of thousands of generations of development, yet the Kalandans had not progressed beyond their ruthless origins. Tasm was most similar to Losira in this regard.

With that, Kirk realized he had let his cultural expectations of physical refinement affect his opinion of Tasm. Suddenly his concerns took on a new complexity. He had to be able to trust his own judgment, yet he had already jumped to conclusions about them. How far could he trust his doubts about these new Kalandans?

His deliberations were interrupted by a call from the *Enterprise*. *"Captain, Mr. Spock is transporting down to the outpost along with Second Officer Kad. You asked to be notified."*

Kirk acknowledged, looking at Losira a moment longer. But he didn't want to be discovered and held accountable by Commander Tasm. He would lose an edge in their already tricky diplomatic negotiations.

So he slipped into the crew quarters until Spock, Kad, and Marl passed by, pushing the new computer suspended by anti-grav units. They were going to try to reactivate the portal.

Kirk knew it was the perfect time for a hard game of anti-grav handball. His yeoman wouldn't mind being woken up in the middle of the night—not much, anyway. And she had nearly beaten him last time, so he would have to look sharp. Maybe if he cleared everything out of himself, physically and mentally, he would have a new perspective. Then he could have a fresh look at these Kalandans.

Chapter Thirteen

SCOTTY LIKED WORKING with Officer Marl. Except for the lurid stripes over his eyes, the Kalandan engineer was an ordinary humanoid. A real nice, obliging guy.

Together they dismantled the cylindrical unit from the old computer bank and shifted it closer to the floor. The monofilaments extended with only a slight pressure, so Scotty slowly moved the cylinder over to the massive arch. They constructed a bracket to attach the cylinder directly to the new computer that was resting at the base.

Mr. Spock and Officer Kad were attaching the monofilaments from the cylinder to the subprocessor. They rarely spoke as they went about the methodical and exacting work of joining each monofilament to the optical data network of the subprocessor.

Marl was an excellent engineer, but he was a bit clumsy in the hands and feet. They couldn't afford to break any monofilaments through a careless misstep. So for safety's sake, Scotty installed a square casing over the monofilaments that ran from the power junction to the cylindrical unit that was now secured to the computer. The long monofilaments that had originally stretched between the arch and the cylinder lay coiled next to the subprocessor.

There was nothing more they could do with the portal until Spock finished attaching the new computer. So Scotty and Marl had another go at the stasis seal over the power junction. But the magnetic flux couldn't be measured, which told them something about the magnitude of the power they could tap.

Since his tricorder couldn't penetrate beyond the diburnium and osmium layers in the walls of the chamber, Scotty turned to the open sections of flooring. Marl was the one who suggested it, diving in to use the maser-saw. Starting near the other foot of the arch, Marl opened the plasticized osmium sheeting to reveal a neutronium beam lying across the base of the arch.

Further exploration revealed the beam was as wide and thick as the arch, about half a meter, and ran underneath the flooring to join the other side of the arch. The arch was really an enclosed neutronium rectangle. The base was supported by diburnium-osmium structural beams.

Under most of the top layer of flooring, throughout the chamber, there were crisscrossing conduits for monofilaments. Scotty traced the bundles leading from the computer to the node overhead. More bundles disappeared into the wall. Certain monofilaments, most likely leading straight to the entrance chamber above, were nearly all fused.

So Scotty went back to the floor, rooting around until he found an empty section where they could get to the final layer of diburnium-osmium alloy.

This layer consisted of thick plates. Scotty unsealed the edges of one plate and pried it up.

He almost dropped it in surprise. Below was a shimmering blue forcefield. The energy discharge distorted the air above it. A loud humming filled the room.

At first it looked continuous, like the security shields in the brig. But as his eyes grew accustomed to the brightness, he could see the series of interlocking octagonal superconductors that formed the matrix below the forcefield.

Spock and Kad joined them. The blue glow reflected on their faces. "What is *that?*" Officer Kad asked.

"A forcefield layer," Scotty said proudly. "Isn't she a beaut?"

"That would explain the energized ions in the diburnium-osmium alloy," Spock commented.

"Aye, and why the sensors canna penetrate below the first level of this station," Scotty agreed.

Aiming his tricorder at the exposed matrix, he recorded a tremendous power reading. The superconductors were creating a number of special forcefields that oscillated in overlapping patterns.

"It's made of keiyurium and silicon animide, fueled by magnetic taps," Scotty said.

Kad was taking his own readings. "The forcefields probably aid in the transformation of geomagnetic energy into power. I worked on a magnetic-flux generator back home, and it's augmented by forcefields of this magnitude."

Marl nodded. "It helps if the forcefields are layered in successive levels, as they seem to be on this station."

Scotty was impressed. "Geomagnetic field generators are tricky machines. What else do your people use them for?"

"We don't build them this big anymore," Marl said ruefully. "Mainly we use the magnetomotive for supplying power to our experimental stations."

Kad finished taking his readings and returned to work on the subprocessor along with Spock.

Marl lowered his own sensor padd closer to the hole. But as he keyed in some command, the thin padd shifted sideways and slipped from his fingers.

Scotty caught it with one hand just before it hit the open forcefield. "Watch what you're doing there, lad!"

Marl's hand was shaking as he accepted the padd back. "If the magnetic flux generator is as large as we think—it could have blown up this entire chamber. . . ." The Kalandan shuddered to think they had come that close to disaster. "Your quick reflexes are much appreciated."

"No need to mention it," Scotty assured him. "We'll just tack this back down." With a few quick spot welds, the heavy-duty plate of diburnium-osmium alloy was placed back over the forcefield.

Scotty thought it was best not to inform Marl's superior officer of the near-accident. Marl was a good lad: he had some of the puppy-dog ways of John Watkins. Watkins used to follow Scotty around, and was always so eager to please.

Besides, Scotty wasn't interested in making trouble. He was just satisfied to be able to explain why they couldn't get a transporter lock on the lower levels. The forcefield layers were preventing it.

With that question now settled, Scotty ambled back to the portal. "Have you figured out what these are yet?"

Scotty pointed to the concave curve at one end of the cylinder. The blue neutronium was polished to an iridescent sheen, and he could barely make out a tiny line forming a spiral a thousand layers thick. Because of the superior Kalandan air filtration system, there wasn't a speck of dust on it.

"Unknown at this time," Kad said shortly.

Scotty blinked at his concise reply. He sounded remarkably like Mr. Spock.

Without fanfare, Spock announced, "I am activating the subprocessor. Mr. Scott, would you please monitor the power flux in the monofilaments?"

"Sure, let's fire her up!" Scotty removed the casing he had put over the monofilaments. Marl assisted, moving carefully this time. Scotty gave the lad an encouraging wink.

Spock stood next to Officer Kad, ready to initiate the subprocessor. "The current default program is a self-diagnostic stimulator. Whatever programming is hardwired within the components of the device will activate the appropriate response."

"We're ready." Scotty crouched next to the monofilaments, the laser wand in place. He detected minimal power levels inside the monofilaments.

"Powering on." Mr. Spock activated the plasma unit that ran the subprocessor. The preliminary sequence began to run.

Kad had the microfocus sensor pressed against the port into the cylinder. "There's activity in the cryostatic junction nodes."

The floor rumbled slightly.

"Power levels rising!" Scotty braced himself against the shaking until it died down. "Up twenty percent . . ."

Next to him, Marl was muttering, confirming his findings with his own laser wand.

Spock read the activity on the screen. "Interfacing with local system. Accessing artificial intelligence routines."

"It's working!" Scotty exclaimed.

Grinning up at Spock, he saw the archway behind the two men as they leaned over the subprocessor. It had gone cloudy.

"Look out!" Scott dropped the laser wand.

Spock turned, holding out his tricorder. The center of the portal was forming into a multireflective vortex. Scotty grabbed his own tricorder to take readings. The clouds were caused by the vaporization of the air on either side of the arch.

Then something started to appear. Three figures stepping away from them, one right after the other. They seemed to appear within the threshold of the portal, yet it gave the illusion of much greater depth.

"That's Losira!" Scott recognized her from the message he had seen. Her uniform left her back mostly bare, with only a narrow strip of purple up the middle, exposing her shoulders and the curve of her waist. He knew she was deadly, yet was somehow vulnerable looking.

The image seemed frozen, with the first figure of Losira stepping on the heels of the second, while the third was almost completely gone except for her raised heel and one arm.

"What is it?" Marl asked, voicing Scotty's own confusion.

Spock was perfectly calm, while Kad was almost as impassive. To Scotty, the only reassuring thing was that the Losira replicas were walking *away* from everyone.

"It appears to be a resonance echo." Spock finished examining his readings. "This was apparently the last task the portal performed."

"Three Losiras," Scotty said. "When you beamed down, Mr. Spock, there were three Losira replicas, weren't there?"

"That is correct, Mr. Scott. One replica for each of the surviving landing party members."

"So this portal sent them," Kad said. "Does that mean it could start sending out more killer replicas?"

Scotty was concerned. "The Losira replica sabotaged the *Enterprise* when it was still a thousand light-years away."

"Agreed; however that requires the use of the directional node, which has been destroyed." Spock put his hand against the computer bank. "Somewhere in this defense computer exists the capability of creating corporeal replicas that can kill with a touch."

"Maybe it's time to crack open some of those modules." Marl was looking at the computer with a speculative zeal that Scotty didn't like.

"Nobody here needs to access such terrible technology." Scotty put a calming hand on the lad's shoulder.

Spock checked the progress of the subprocessor. "The unit has initiated a top level diagnostic. Once that is completed, we can test the portal."

"It's going t' work, Mr. Spock, I just know it!" Scotty didn't mind Spock's tendency to be skeptical. With the help of the Kalandans, they were going to do it. He would bet a bottle of Romulan ale that the portal would be operational within hours.

Scotty was still grinning as he took another look at the retreating Losira replicas. "But you never know, lads. You better keep an eye on that arch to make sure nothing else comes out of it."

Marl started eyeing the arch with renewed suspicion, as Scotty clapped his hands together. "I'm going to report to th' captain. He could use a bit o' good news."

Tasm had rejoined Captain Kirk in the command center to question Losira. Kirk was in the chair, leading their current session. Overall, he seemed increasingly suspicious toward her. He had not allowed her to get any closer to him than within arm's length. She had pushed it until he rebuffed her, just to be sure, then abandoned seduction as a potential ploy. Obviously this male was not as susceptible to feminine wiles as she had first thought.

Kirk started to ask Losira, "Could you give us a sample of your genetic—"

"Why do you want that?" Tasm interrupted.

"A genetic sample could tell us a great deal about the Kalandans. You know that. Aren't you interested in it?"

"Our genetic makeup is no concern of yours. I believe you're asking because you don't trust us." She tried to sound gravely disappointed, as Losira sometimes did. Like she was lovingly guiding an errant child.

"Don't *you* trust *us*?" Kirk countered.

Tasm couldn't ignore his doubt. She was going to have to brazen this through. "Of course we trust you. We have done nothing but cooperate with you. By all means, ask the replica for a copy of our genetic code."

Once again Tasm was saved by Losira's evasive answer, "That information is controlled by the defense computer." Apparently the Kalandans were well-versed with biological weapons and knew better than to freely toss their DNA around.

Just then, Kad arrived with his report on a padd. She quickly scanned it as Engineer Scott verbally gave his report to Captain Kirk. Scott was talking about seeing the Losira replicas again.

Tasm was more interested in Kad's report. Marl had investigated the arch, as she had ordered, and found that the neutronium was superficially attached to the structural supports of the station. It appeared the entire arch could be lifted with an anti-grav gurney. If it were turned on its side, it would fit through the corridors. They could push the archway to the top level where they could then transport it onto their ship.

The only problem was the Starfleet ship. With Kirk's growing distrust, she didn't think she could convince him to let her take the portal. Not without a fight. But the replicators were almost finished with the two quantum torpedoes. Then she would take the portal, with or without Kirk's agreement.

"Keep me informed," she ordered Kad. "I want to be there when you test the portal."

Kad agreed, turning smartly to go back down the long corridor to the computer chamber. Tasm was very pleased with his work. She had observed him interacting with Commander Spock, and their rapport was exceptional. Marl had also manipulated Engineer Scott into taking a protective role with him.

Kirk had turned out to be trickier than she had anticipated. So she had prepared another plan of action. It would be Kirk's last chance to surrender the portal.

With the six members of the other pod working on search teams, and Luz still sealed in her cell, that left only Mlan and Pir to work on Tasm's special weapon. It was a tractor-projector they had acquired on one of their first engagements, not long after they had left their birthing world. Using a tractor emitter, the projector would create an interference pattern on a distant focal point. They could set the pattern so that sensors would read it as two Klingon battleships on an attack approach.

Captain Kirk knew that Klingons were coming. He would believe it long enough to evacuate the station and notify Starfleet Command. If he didn't leave in the face of certain Klingon attack, she would disable and, if possible, destroy the *Enterprise* using their quantum torpedoes. By the time any other ships arrived, it would be too late. She would be well on her way home with the interstellar transporter.

She took the opportunity during Kirk's discussion with his chief engineer to check with Mlan on board their ship. "Report," she ordered through the padd.

Mlan's report flowed over the screen—the notched symbols that indicated the tractor-projector was ready to be deployed. Since it was better to place the tractor-projector far away from the target, Tasm decided to place it strategically on the surface of the planetoid. They could engage a course change—claim there was Klingon debris or something—and beam the unit down to the southern pole. The *Enterprise* wouldn't be able to detect it from their equatorial orbit.

It would take three of her pod-mates to deploy the tractor-projector in the window of time they would have during a minor course change. Tasm knew she would have to unseal Luz from her cell.

"Carry on, Scotty," Kirk finally said to his officer.

Scotty nodded uncertainly at his captain. Apparently he couldn't understand why Kirk was so dour when everything was going smoothly. Tasm had to give Kirk credit. He was not an easy dupe. He had nothing concrete to go on, but he persisted in doubting her.

"I'm needed back on my ship." Tasm pocketed her padd, glad of an excuse to end this unproductive session.

Kirk seemed surprised that she would leave him alone with the Losira replica. But she preferred him to concentrate on questioning the replica rather than questioning what she was doing.

Their ruse had almost played out. It was successful, despite the contradictions that had inevitably arose. Their cover as Kalandans only needed to hold for a short while longer.

The portal would soon be tested, and the quantum torpedoes were almost ready. After that, no one, not even Captain Kirk, would be able to stop her.

Chapter Fourteen

DR. MCCOY KNEW that progress was being made down on the station, while he spent too much time conducting a long-needed meeting between the botany staff and his medical technicians. McCoy tried to be positive, congratulating them on working well together on the sporophyte virus as they drew up protocol to use in future investigations. The fact that they didn't discover the vaccine on their own was a moot point, as he told Dr. Es. For the moment he had succeeded in avoiding a tour of her lab space, and merely agreed they all needed more room.

Everything paled in comparison to the Kalandans and their station. McCoy could understand why the captain stayed down there. Jim was better off in the thick of the activity. Even he found it unnerving not being directly involved, when they knew the Klingons were bearing down on their position.

McCoy called up the search team roster to see who was going down to the station next. Luz was assigned as one of the Kalandan searchers, so he immediately signed himself up to be on her team, booting off the luckless Ensign Chekov, who had also volunteered. Sometimes rank had its privileges.

As the search teams introduced themselves in the upper chamber and started down to the living quarters, McCoy fell in beside Luz. She was pleasant, but a bit withdrawn.

"Are you all right?" he asked.

Her eyes shifted. "Working too hard, I suppose."

McCoy knew there was something more, but he felt constrained from probing her. These Kalandans were private people. They didn't talk a lot about themselves.

It was the same as they went about cataloguing the personal items in each of the rooms. Luz wasn't like the Kalandans on the other teams, who seemed to be in high spirits. They chatted with the Starfleet officers as they scanned the objects. He could sometimes hear them talking in the corridors before entering another room.

The more of Luz McCoy saw, the more he liked her. She sat on the bed, her head bent as she held the scanner to a small flat icon taken from a container. Her fingers held it delicately, almost reverently. The hollows in her cheeks were filled with shadows, and her forehead was tight with some worry. She seemed defenseless somehow.

"Why are you so sad?" McCoy sat on a bench near her.

Luz looked up, her light brown hair falling back from her face. "Don't you think this is sad?" She lifted her hand at the empty room. "We live, but only for a wink in time. Then we are dead, and everything we thought and dreamed and hoped is gone with us."

"At least we leave behind what we've accomplished," McCoy said gently, seeing that she was truly distressed.

"The scientists left this behind." Luz gestured to the compact container of useless and unidentifiable objects.

"It's hard to know why these things had emotional significance," McCoy admitted. "But there might be patterns that the individual search teams can't see. Besides, you're forgetting this station itself. This place is a remarkable accomplishment."

Luz shrugged and tried to smile. "I'm being over-emotional again, I know. My . . . crewmates would say it's my worst trait."

"Well, I prefer people who are in touch with their emotions. There are some people who want to go through life feeling nothing! I don't understand it, myself. Especially when they take such a high and mighty attitude, like they're better than us because we feel joy and sorrow. . . ."

"That's exactly it." Her eyes were shining. "I feel defective sometimes, but I know I'm not."

McCoy frowned at the idea of those plodding Kalandans making her feel bad. He had seen that officer working with Spock, and he acted just like a Vulcan. All work and no time for any pleasantries.

Luz sighed. "If I died tomorrow, I wouldn't leave enough behind to fill even this small container. There would be literally nothing left of me."

McCoy felt awful. She seemed lost and unhappy, with no one but a stranger—an alien being—to talk to.

How could he complain about his life compared to hers? He reached out to pat her hand, awkwardly feeling like an older brother or uncle. She was very attractive, with her slightly upturned nose, but he no longer felt romantically inclined toward her.

Which made it worse when Captain Kirk appeared in the doorway and saw them in that intimate pose. McCoy started, letting go of her hand.

"I hope I'm not interrupting anything." Kirk gave McCoy a penetrating look.

That flustered him even more. "Of course not! We were just cataloguing items . . . You know Dr. Luz, Captain."

"Nice to see you again." Kirk sauntered into the room, glancing around at the barrenness. "Ensign Chekov complained that he had been bumped off the duty roster by you. Now I see why."

McCoy thought there was no need for him to be so smug. "I find this station as interesting as you do, Jim. I see you've been working after duty-shift, too."

Kirk's eyes slid to Luz. "I'm trying to learn more about the Kalandans. Perhaps you wouldn't mind telling me a few things."

"Whatever you'd like to know." Luz looked up with composure.

Kirk was quite serious. "How far back do your records go?"

"We have data fragments that go back fifteen thousand years, but nothing substantial until after the age of darkness ended three thousand years ago."

"That's what Commander Tasm said." Kirk smiled slightly. "If you only have fragments, how did you recognize the signal that was sent by this station?"

Luz readily answered, "We detected the extreme energy burst, which carried an identification tag of the station and commander."

"That's what Commander Tasm said," Kirk repeated.

"Well, then!" McCoy was irritated by Jim's overtly suspicious attitude. "Maybe that's because it's the truth."

Kirk glanced at McCoy. "Bones, what I meant was— that's *exactly* what Commander Tasm said. Word for word. Like it came out of some kind of manual."

Luz was sitting there, her mouth tightly closed. It was her hands that bothered McCoy, the fingers gripping each other so tightly that her knuckles darkened.

"I just asked several other Kalandans on the search teams, and they told me the same thing." Kirk stepped closer to Luz, lowering his voice. "Your entire crew has been given some kind of party line of what you can and can't say—isn't that true?"

"No," she quickly denied, getting up from the bed. Her arms crossed in front of her. "How could you think that?"

"Because that's what's happening. But I think you're different. You can tell us the truth."

"I'm not different!" She looked to McCoy for support. "It's just that I have to work harder to try to be like the others, or they bother me about it."

McCoy knew she was alluding to their conversation, and he felt compelled to step in. Her body language was screaming for help. "Come on, Jim. I don't think we gain anything by badgering our allies like this. . . ."

"You, too, Bones?" Kirk stared at him.

"You're being confrontational." McCoy felt aggravated, but he tried to restrain his reaction in front of

Luz. "Here we are working together. I think it's time you stop acting like we're enemies!"

For a moment, McCoy wondered if he had over-stepped the boundaries of rank. He was good friends with the captain, and sometimes they disagreed, but McCoy felt sure Kirk knew that he would back up any decision he made.

Kirk wasn't too pleased, but before he could reply, his communicator beeped. Frowning, he flipped it open. "Kirk here."

"Spock here, Captain. We are prepared to run a test of the portal."

Kirk nodded shortly. "Very good, Mr. Spock. We'll be right there."

McCoy was relieved by the interruption. "I'm going with you. If anything is being tested, you'll need a doctor on hand." He glanced at Luz. "Two doctors."

Luz noticed that Captain Kirk readily gave in to Dr. McCoy's suggestion. She had apparently managed to suborn a significant target. McCoy was clearly second only to Kirk, if that.

The fact that she had done so well with McCoy gave her a boost of confidence. There was nothing like the agony of four hundred crons of the information feed to motivate a person.

It was Tasm's fault she had repeated exactly the same words forced into her through the information feed. They had fallen from her lips without conscious control. That just showed how dumb Tasm could be. And the others for blindly reciting the information they had been given.

The pain of being sealed in the cell for so long, unable to stand or move about . . . it gnawed at her. Normally they spent a few dozen crons at the most meditating in their cells. The aftereffects of the prolonged feed made her less charming and inviting toward Dr. McCoy. But as it turned out, her fragile state had served to bond him more deeply to her.

Luz had managed to work out the most severe of her release shakes during their covert mission to deploy the tractor-projector. Another one of Tasm's disastrous decisions, in Luz's opinion. It was so predictable. Tasm had used the tractor-projector on every engagement for which she had been leader.

Luz doubted the tractor-projector would work to repel the Starfleet vessel. She was sure the *Enterprise* would stay and defend the station at all costs. It was inevitable that they would discover the tractor-projector. Tasm would lose any trust they had gained, and it would accomplish nothing.

But Luz hadn't said a word against the plan, biting her tongue the entire time they deployed the tractor-projector. She didn't want to risk being sealed in her cell again. She would do almost anything to keep that from happening.

Luz and Dr. McCoy took a place along the back wall just as Tasm arrived in the portal chamber. Tasm looked as if she wanted to order Luz back up to the scout ship. But Luz was with her target, and it gave them an equal number of Petraw and Starfleet officers. Tasm's reasoning was as clear as if she spoke out loud.

Marl also stood near his target, the Starfleet engineer, while Kad and Spock were working next to the portal. The shiny blue cylinder had been jury-rigged to a Starfleet subprocessor that had been placed next to one base of the arch.

Captain Kirk stepped closer with a speculative look. "Is this arch responsible for transporting the *Enterprise* a thousand light-years away, Mr. Spock?"

"Unknown, Captain. Due to the neutronium casing of the components, we have been limited to studying only the power and computer interface hardware."

Kad straightened, looking over at Tasm. "The arch itself receives direct power from the geomagnetic generator, and apparently serves to channel the magnetic current initiated by the cylinder."

"Just don't ask us how it works," Scotty added from the other side of the arch.

Spock didn't glance in the direction of their outspoken engineer. "Our flexible diagnostic program has matched sequences with the cylindrical unit, supplying responses depending on the queries it has issued. We believe the unit can be activated with minimal risk."

Tasm crossed her arms. "What is risk compared to the reward we have before us?"

Kirk shook his head shortly. "We've seen other examples of superior alien technology capable of relocating objects in space. They are not to be taken lightly."

Next to Luz, McCoy suddenly spoke up. "Yes, the Metrons, the Gamesters of Triskelion, and the Preservers' Obelisk on Miramanee's planet all used some form of dimensional transporter." He swallowed hard before adding, "And of course the Guardian of Forever, which was capable of moving objects in time as well as in space."

"Correct, Doctor," Spock agreed. "However, we lack data to ascertain whether this alien technology relates to any of those other transporters. It does not appear to be consistent with the Kalandan technology we have thus far examined on this station."

Kirk nodded. "Understood, Mr. Spock. Let's see for ourselves what it can do."

Tasm gave a sharp assent, revealing too much of her eagerness in Luz's opinion. It was not helpful to betray any weakness to the opposing side in an engagement.

Indeed, Spock raised one brow toward Tasm before turning back to the computer. He and Kad adjusted a few of the controls.

"Activating the unit," Spock announced.

There was a pause, then the archway started to fill with a cloudy mist.

The planetoid rumbled, just a slight tremor that soon faded.

"That's what happened before!" the Starfleet engineer cried out. "Then we saw those three Losira replicas walking through th' portal—"

"Look!" Captain Kirk interrupted, gesturing to one side of the arch.

Something was happening to the cylinder. Luz crowded forward along with the others to get a better look. A holographic sphere now rested in the concave top of the cylinder. Tiny laser crosslines bisecting the sphere made it look like a standard targeting interface. Then she couldn't see anything more because Marl stepped in front of her.

Amid the exclamations and speculations at the appearance of the ghostly sphere, Luz focused on Tasm's jubilant gloating. "It *is* an interstellar transporter! We must get it functional again."

That was apparently the consensus. Spock and Kad

agreed that activating the computer had initiated the targeting mechanism. There was further speculation that the destroyed computer nodes in the ceiling overhead had served to pinpoint the portal's target on the surface of the Kalandan station.

"While we can no longer perform an intraplanetary transport," Spock finally summed up, "it may be possible to open this portal to another planet."

"Do it, Spock," Kirk ordered. "Set the coordinates for Earth."

Luz approved of Kirk's way with command. That was what Tasm lacked. Luz was almost pleased at the way Tasm was biting her lip. She couldn't protest Kirk's choice of target, not when they couldn't reveal the location of any planets in Petraw territory.

Spock took some time performing calculations with his tricorder, then he adjusted the targeting sphere. Kirk watched his science officer closely, as did Kad. Luz could tell that Kad had come to deeply respect the Vulcan.

Spock moved the final laser line into place. "Earth, Captain."

Luz held her breath as she stared at the arch. The mist boiled, making everyone tense in expectation. Finally it started to clear. Gold appeared first in the center. It spread to the edges of the portal, revealing a golden sweep of rolling land. The image sharpened and stretched back to the horizon of a sky so deep blue that Luz thought the color must be distorted.

"Iowa!" Kirk exclaimed softly. His hand reached out and he took two steps forward. "Spock! It isn't . . ."

"It is Iowa, Captain."

"Mr. Spock!" Spock didn't react as Kirk beamed at

him, then gave a disbelieving laugh. "It's so real, so close, almost as if I can smell the wheat . . ."

Kirk took one step forward as if compelled.

Spock's quiet voice broke the spell. "Do not go through, Captain. We do not know if it will safely transport material objects without the Kalandan defense computer."

Kirk reluctantly pulled away. Luz wanted to shout at him, to urge him to go on. She couldn't believe it was true. An interstellar transporter! A true gateway through space.

Tasm also seemed elated. "Let me try," she insisted.

Kirk hesitated, taking one more look at the waving, golden vegetation. Then he smiled at Mr. Spock as they both moved back, giving their allies a change to operate the portal.

Tasm went right up to the arch, flushed with importance. "Target our ship, Kad. We can send something through to see if it works."

Kad reached out to touch the targeting sphere and the view through the portal quickly faded to misty white. But after Kad set the coordinates, only vague impressions of light gray emerged in the portal before quickly vanishing again.

Spock went to assist, concentrating on the Starfleet display on the subprocessor. Kad checked the diagnostic readouts. "Perhaps the electroplasmic device in your bag is disrupting the interface sensors of the targeting sphere."

Tasm immediately unbelted her work-pouch and gave it to him. Kad passed it on to Marl. Luz automatically stepped forward when Marl, in some instinctive response to get the pouch as far from the portal as possible, handed it back to her.

Luz retreated almost to the doorway clutching Tasm's precious pouch. She could feel the lumpy sides as it dangled from its strap slung over her shoulder. If Tasm saw her with it, she would order Marl to get it back. The pouch held Tasm's padd, the key to her command logs during this engagement.

The pouch also held the initiator for the tractor-projector unit—the only electroplasmic device Kad could have been referring to. Luz thought she recognized the edge of the unit peeking up from the corner where the flap of the pouch was pulled back. Soon Tasm was going to try her absurd Klingon feint using the tractor-projector, and that would destroy any hopes they had of getting away with the portal.

Tasm was asking Kad questions as Spock helped him adjust the targeting sphere. But the mist in the portal didn't clear.

Kirk looked amused. "Having trouble getting it to listen to you?"

Tasm ignored Kirk, demanding, "What's wrong with it?"

Mr. Spock theorized, "It is possible that because this portal is powered by the magnetic field of the planetoid, you must target another planet in order to balance the dimensional transport."

"Brilliant as ever, Mr. Spock," Kirk told him. "Set the coordinates for Earth again, and target Starfleet Academy. We'll send something through, then find out if it arrived safely."

In the bustle to prepare for the test, Luz reached into the pouch and keyed a few commands into the initiator. It was already set to imitate Klingon vessels in an interactive attack pattern. She increased the deflection bounce to show three ships approaching instead of two. That should throw Tasm off long enough to cause a diversion. Tactically that's what the projector deflector was good for—a brief diversion that would soon be discovered.

But that was all Luz needed. She didn't intend to let Tasm ruin this engagement and lose the interstellar transporter. If Tasm wouldn't do what was clearly right, then Luz would have to.

She pressed the button on the initiator, sending a time-delay sequence to the tractor-projector. Then she cleared the memory. Tasm wasn't very bright. She wouldn't realize what had happened until it was too late. By then, Luz would already be on their birthing world with the portal.

After all, what better way to take this technology back to their birthing world than to use the portal to get it there?

Luz called Marl away from the crowd around the portal. She handed the pouch back to him, and putting a shaking hand to her head, she murmured, "I need to return to the ship. Overload on the information feed." She was twitching convincingly, reacting to what she had just done.

Information-feed overload was a malady that often appeared after intensive sessions. Marl nodded sympathetically. *Brainless fool,* she thought.

Luz managed to slip from the computer chamber without anyone else seeing her go, including Dr. McCoy, who was intent on the portal. That was good. She was done with them. Soon she would be back on her birthing world, being praised and rewarded for her ingenuity in saving the interstellar transporter.

Her anticipation was so high she couldn't stop trembling. She would finally become what she deserved. At the very least, she would never have to see her podmates again. She would never again be sealed in her cell for forced information feed. She would never again have to bow down to pettiness and incompetence. She would be hailed as a savior by all Petraw.

Chapter Fifteen

CAPTAIN KIRK DECIDED to send a tricorder through the portal to Starfleet Academy. Spock programmed a message into the tricorder that would automatically play when it was activated. Kirk also ordered Uhura to send a subspace message to the Academy informing them of the imminent arrival of the tricorder.

Then Kirk once again took his place in front of the archway. With the programmed tricorder in one hand, he watched as Spock set the coordinates. His first officer's hands moved surely this time, repeating nearly the same sequence as the first time. Kirk had been surprised when Spock had targeted his home state of Iowa, but he had also appreciated the gesture.

Slowly the boiling clouds began to clear from the portal, revealing red rocky cliffs that abruptly narrowed around the rough waters of San Francisco Bay. Spanning the coastlines was the ancient and still spectacular Golden Gate Bridge.

For a moment, Kirk couldn't speak. His perspective

was high and disorienting until he realized the portal was showing the view from the small terrace outside the commandant's office. It was on the third floor, overlooking the buildings of Starfleet Academy.

"Right on target, Mr. Spock." Kirk gave him a disbelieving shake of his head.

"Of course, Captain." Spock seemed unimpressed with his own achievement.

McCoy exclaimed at the familiar sight, and Scotty was muttering his pleasure at seeing the view that was so beloved by all Starfleet cadets.

There was a hazy quality to the air that Kirk had almost forgotten. Yet the colors were dramatic, refracted by the moisture on every surface. Even the flagstones of the terrace gleamed in the soft afternoon light. Benches lined the railing, with small pots of evergreens echoing the trees on the surrounding hillsides.

Kirk leaned forward and tossed the tricorder through the portal. It hung for a few moments in the arch as if caught between the boundary of dimensions.

The floor of the station trembled under his feet, growing stronger. A flashing light briefly obscured the portal, while pink and red glints sparked off the blue archway. Kirk stumbled to one side as the planetoid heaved then settled.

Then the tricorder continued its arch out the other side of the portal. It landed on the flagstones and slid a short way.

"What was that tremor?" Kirk demanded.

Scotty was monitoring the system with his tricorder. "The passage through th' portal caused a magnetic sweep and a forty-three percent power surge, Captain. I bet th' geomagnetic synch is no longer aligned with th' natural declination of th' planetoid."

"Agreed," Spock said. "That could cause fluctuations in the power feed and affect the stability of the dipolar magnetic field."

"Could that interfere with a safe transport?"

"Unknown, Captain."

It looked so real on the other side of the arch that Kirk itched to try it. The tricorder lay there, almost within reach. It seemed like it had survived the journey with no ill effects . . . but even he couldn't do it. If the portal worked, he would be stuck light-years away from the *Enterprise*.

Kirk was also familiar with temporal accidents after his visit to a certain parallel universe. It was dangerously easy to pass through time and dimensions without intending to.

His communicator beeped, and he reluctantly pulled away from the portal. "Kirk here."

Lt. Sulu sounded worried. *"Captain, our long-range sensors are detecting vessels approaching. According to the energy signature, it's Klingons."*

"Klingons!" McCoy exclaimed in alarm. "I thought they wouldn't arrive until tomorrow."

Kirk spoke into his communicator, "Are you sure, Mr. Sulu?"

"Aye, Captain. I confirmed it with Officer Mlan of the Kalandan ship."

"Red alert, Mr. Sulu. Stand by phaser banks."

"Aye, sir!"

Kirk turned to see Commander Tasm digging into her pouch and coming up with a handheld device. She stared at it for a few moments, shaking her head slightly as she shoved it back inside. "How many Klingon ships are there?" she demanded.

Kirk repeated the question to Sulu, who replied. *"Three, Captain."*

"Three," Tasm repeated, sounding worried herself.

"How long before they arrive?" Kirk asked.

"According to the computer, nineteen minutes forty-three seconds, sir."

That didn't leave much time. The others were frozen, looking from him to the portal.

Kirk ordered Sulu, "Alert the search teams and begin transporting them off the station."

"Aye, sir!" Sulu acknowledged before signing off.

Kirk folded his communicator, turning to Dr. McCoy. "Go make sure the search teams get off, then transport up to the *Enterprise* yourself."

"What about you?" McCoy asked.

Kirk glanced at Spock and Scotty. "We have to figure out a way to secure this portal. Our orders are to not let it fall into Klingon hands."

"We should remove the portal from the station," Tasm agreed. "I am loath to desecrate anything here, but the portal must be protected."

Spock raised one brow. "It will take approximately fifty-three minutes to remove the restraining bolts attaching the arch to the substructure of the station."

"Too long," Kirk muttered. He eyed the cylindrical unit and subprocessor. They could sever the monofilaments that united the cylinder to the archway and power source, then remove it to the *Enterprise*. But he would rather not do something so destructive. It had taken hours for Spock and Kad to attach the monofilaments just from the cylinder to the subprocessor.

Tasm clearly expected that she would take the portal onto her own ship for protection. She certainly wouldn't agree to let them hold part of it on board the *Enterprise*. So he didn't mention the option of cutting the cylinder off.

"Too bad my shield didn't work," Scotty spoke up, "or we could hide the entrance."

Tasm raised her head. "We have a shield that could conceal the entrance."

Kirk hesitated. But he could see no other viable option. "Very well. Get your shield in place. Mr. Spock, you and Scotty stay here and dismantle the archway."

Commander Tasm ordered Officer Kad, "Tell Mlan to send down the Teleris shield."

"Teleris shield?" Spock asked, curious and perhaps even a bit jealous.

Kirk held up his hand. "The question is, will it work?"

"It will," Tasm said flatly.

Kirk made sure that he was the last one out of the station, leaving only Marl and Kad down in the portal chamber with Spock and Scotty. They were already dismantling the arch from the station.

On the surface, he watched Commander Tasm set up the shield unit with assistance from Officer Pir. It was much larger than Scotty's shield, and was painted an ominous black.

But when they stepped back and it was activated, Kirk could instantly see the difference. The unit disappeared, but nothing else seemed different. There was no subliminal hum or tension in the air. No burning smell.

"Looks good," he told Tasm.

She nodded shortly. "Are you prepared to fight to protect this station?"

"Commander, since we discovered this station I haven't stopped fighting to protect it." He refrained from adding, "Even from you." Kirk returned her nod, then signaled the *Enterprise* to beam him up.

Luz stayed hidden in the living quarters near the main corridor, knowing that the first chambers had been searched already. Impatiently she waited through the general cry which called for the searchers to immediately vacate the station.

Footsteps ran past, and there were hurried calls to one another. Since Luz was close to the corridor, she overheard Kad explaining to their pod-mates that they were going to erect the Teleris shield to conceal the entrance while they dismantled the arch from the station.

So . . . Tasm had prevailed thus far upon Captain Kirk. But when he found out that the Klingon ships were fake, that would undermine everything Tasm had worked for. Her plan was flawed in its conception.

Luz was breathless with hope. She was going home! After a lifetime of gazing at the stars, trying to find the tiny sun that blazed down on the desiccated crust of her birthing world . . . she was going home as she had longed to. The portal was a sign set in her path, calling for her return. And she was the only one who could see the perfect use for it.

Luz waited until there were no more sounds, then she quickly ran up the corridor. It was not enough to count on the tractor-projector for a delay. She would take no chances on being caught before she had used the portal to return home.

There were a few details of her plan for escape that were still undetermined—such as what she was going to do about the men who were dismantling the portal. But, carried away by her grand passion to return to her birthing world, she was convinced that everything would fall into place. She was doing the right thing, so it had to work.

Pausing carefully in the oval nexus chamber, she listened before looking down the corridor. The botany labs were empty, as was the entrance chamber at the top.

Luz waited a few moments more to be sure that Tasm had returned to their ship. Then she went through the U-shaped corridor to stand before the door. It slid up smoothly, then the rock slab moved aside.

There it was: the bulky Teleris shield. It had been acquired a generation ago, and every Petraw ship carried one. Luz knew several ways to subvert the command lock on the shield so that it would open to no one but her.

Unfolding her padd to full extension, she crouched next to the shield and inserted the tab into the port. When she was done, the shield would not drop unless it received a command from her personal padd. Luz worked fast.

Chapter Sixteen

STRIDING ONTO THE BRIDGE of the *Enterprise,* Kirk took command from Mr. Sulu. "Report."

"Sir! The Klingon battleships are entering this sector. They'll be within hailing range in eight minutes."

Sulu took the helm again, as Kirk slid into the command chair. He knew what was coming. The Klingons were aware that the *'Ong* had been destroyed. They wouldn't care whether it was the Kalandans or the *Enterprise* who had done the deed. Especially if they knew the *'Ong* had been engaged in battle with his ship at the time of its destruction.

Not that it mattered. Kirk knew only too well that Klingons would use any excuse for a fight. At least this time the *Enterprise* was in shape to do battle.

Tasm's panel scrolled the data she needed as the three Klingon vessels neared the planetoid. It was unfortunate that their replicator had only had time to create two quantum torpedoes. They did not have an advantage in this encounter, so it was not the type of fight that scouts usually engaged in.

But strategically, she could still turn it to her benefit. The portal was being dismantled and would soon be removed. And she believed her claim would be strengthened if she could dispatch the Klingons. With two quantum torpedoes, she was confident that she could deal a severe blow to at least two of the vessels. As long as the *Enterprise* dispatched the third battleship, that would clear the field except for the Starfleet ship. And now she had the advantage over Kirk with the station sealed under her shield.

Tasm examined every detail of the Klingons' approach from her panel, along with the condition of her own ship and the *Enterprise.* Kirk had shields on full, with phaser banks fully charged.

Both ships stayed in orbit around the planetoid. It could be tactically useful to be near the surface in a fight. That kind of proximity would help sustain more complex attack patterns. The Petraw navigational computer was up to the task, ready to engage in maneuvers on command.

When she finally had a moment to think of anything other than battle prep, Tasm called one of their other pod-mates. Pir and Mlan were manning the other two stations, so she ordered the pod-mate to check on Luz's condition. Kad had informed her that Luz had returned to the ship due to information-feed overload.

Before Tasm had finished initiating the targeting computer for the quantum torpedoes, their pod-mate contacted the command center. *"Luz isn't in her cell."*

Tasm instantly consulted the interior scanner. Luz was not anywhere on the ship.

"Luz isn't on board. She must still be inside the station," Tasm announced.

Pir looked up, stunned by the verbal announcement. "Maybe she lost consciousness on her way out."

"The search teams would have seen her . . . unless she was hiding," Tasm finished grimly.

She could see the questions in their eyes. They couldn't believe it, because it was contrary to everything they held dear. Luz had stayed in the station, defying orders. It was incomprehensible that one of their pod-mates could be malfunctioning that badly.

What was Luz thinking? Tasm knew her pod-mate had an individualistic streak. Luz wanted to excel, that was certain. But there was no telling why she had stayed on the station.

Tasm notified Marl and Kad through the information feed to their padds. They would see her order to find Luz and restrain her, if necessary, when they next entered data.

Tasm was determined to seal Luz in her cell for the duration of this engagement. If Luz interfered any further, then, for the good of the Petraw, she would have to be put away.

Tasm would deal with that when called upon. Meanwhile, the three Klingon vessels had changed course and were bearing down on them in attack formation. The *Enterprise* was attempting to hail the Klingons with repeated queries that went ignored. It looked like there would be a fight.

With the shield under her control, Luz reentered the station. Now she had gained the time she needed to concentrate on those who stood between her and perfect bliss.

But how?

Casting her eyes down at her padd, she was not sure if there was any way to turn it into a weapon. It was too light to use as a blunt instrument. She looked around the entrance chamber. The lift was still in place under the burnt-out computer node. The medical equipment McCoy had used for his tests had been removed since the Petraw had arrived.

Then she noticed something on the table near the stools used by the Starfleet security guards. Going closer, she saw that it was a full hypospray. Next to it were two extra vials of reddish liquid. It was the vaccine for the sporophyte virus. Apparently a few doses were left here in case anyone's vaccine wore off and they needed another booster before they could be transported back up.

The sporophyte vaccine was dangerous if too many doses were taken. The information feed that Tasm had forced down her brain had repeated the information—which Luz already knew—that a double dose of the vaccine could bring on seizure. A triple doze could cause an irreversible coma.

Sweeping up the loaded hypospray and the two extra vials, Luz hoped that Marl and Kad had recently been given their booster. It would make her attack more effective.

With her weapons in hand, she hurried down the corridor, heading back to the computer chamber.

With anyone but her plodding pod-mates, the distraction wouldn't have worked at all. It simply proved her opinion. If Tasm couldn't figure out that it was their own tractor-projector creating an image of three Klingon battleships, then she wasn't likely to succeed in this engagement.

Luz knew it was up to her to save the interstellar portal for her people.

Chapter Seventeen

LT. UHURA CONTINUED to issue the Starfleet hail on all channels. "Klingon vessels, this is the *Starship Enterprise* of the United Federation of Planets. Please respond!"

Pressing the hail button repeatedly, she was reminded of the way the Kalandan ship had swooped down on them, also without responding. But the Klingon attack by the *'Ong* had been so merciless and their situation so desperate that she couldn't help feeling more confident now that Captain Kirk was back in command. The tension on the bridge was different this time, more expectant and ready rather than apprehensive.

The captain appeared confident, examining the approach pattern of the Klingon battleships. "Change course to bearing three-three-zero mark two-four."

Ensign Chekov acknowledged, "Aye, Captain."

That swung the *Enterprise* out of synchronous equatorial orbit. Uhura continued to repeatedly send their hail.

Lt. Sulu reported, "Captain, I'm reading some un-usual energy emissions coming from the planetoid."

"Is it the shield?" Kirk demanded.

"Negative, Captain. This is something else." Sulu was concentrating on his panel. "It's nowhere near the entrance to the station. The readings are faint. . . ."

Kirk glanced at the Klingon battleships looming closer on the screen. "What is it, Mr. Sulu?"

"Unknown, sir—"

Chekov interrupted, "Captain! The battleships have stopped. They're five hundred thousand kilometers away and holding."

Kirk waited, as they all did, hardly drawing breath. But the Klingons came no closer.

Tasm's ship was prepared, her finger ready on the command to activate the quantum torpedoes. But the Klingon battleships halted just outside weapons range.

Unexpectedly, the sensor feed blinked off, then back on, as if the Klingon ships had blipped out of existence for a micron.

Out of existence . . . Sensors were operating per-fectly . . .

Tasm exclaimed, "There aren't any Klingon ships!"

Both Pir and Mlan were seeing the same sensor read-outs. "What's happening?" Mlan asked.

Tasm dug into her pouch, pulling out the initiator. The program she had created appeared to be in waiting mode. But when she ran a self-diagnostic, the initiator reported the tractor-projector was currently operating.

"It's our own tractor-projector!" Tasm clenched the unit in frustration. "Is there any way we can turn it off from here?"

"We . . . can't," Mlan protested. "Not from here. The initiator only works at close range."

"The *Enterprise* will figure it out soon." Tasm frowned at the illusion of Klingon battleships hovering just out of range. "It must have been Luz!"

Who else would have done such a thing but Luz? Luz who was still down on the station.

Now Tasm would have to convince the *Enterprise* that Luz had deployed the tractor-projector on her own and was running rogue inside the station. Once Luz was captured, she would have to be put away.

Tasm reached out and hailed the *Enterprise*.

Luz crept close to the doorway to the gateway chamber, listening to the low voices as they worked on the arch. Carefully, she eased her eye around the edge of the door. She could see the chopped-up computer bank with the solid row of modules hiding most of the room. But there was movement on the other side, and the top of the arch was in view.

"Back up there, man," Engineer Scott drawled from behind the bank.

Marl stepped back, holding a maser-saw limply in one hand. Luz took the chance and leaned out further. Flicking one hand, she caught his eye. His mouth opened to exclaim her name.

Luz quickly motioned for silence. Then she gestured for him to come over.

Puzzled, he stepped forward for a moment. She wasn't sure if he spoke to Kad. Then Marl rounded the computer bank, coming toward her.

She darted up the corridor, urging him to follow after her.

Marl, the dim-witted, looked eager as he caught up to her in the command center. She headed directly into the corridor leading to the living quarters, trying to put as much distance between them and the portal chamber as possible.

"What's happening?" Marl whispered, unable to wait any longer.

"This is it," Luz said, trying to maneuver to his side. "You need to go up to drop the shield."

"But we're not done yet dismantling—" Marl started to say.

Luz jabbed the hypospray against his neck as she had seen the Starfleet medical technicians do. The vial emptied into his bloodstream.

Marl let out a strangled shriek, spasming. His fingers drew into claws as he gasped for air.

Luz watched nonplussed as he went rigid and fell flat on his face. It was a large vial, made for the heavier Starfleet personnel, so it was probably extra-strong for the Petraw. That was good, since she only had two vials left.

She grabbed Marl's stiff, trembling arm and pulled. It was hard to drag him. He had always been big for a Petraw, more like a defender than a scout. Luz had nothing in particular against Marl. If anything, he was somewhat less irritating than the rest. But she didn't care enough about him to worry whether the vaccine would cause permanent damage.

Once she got Marl moving, it was easier to slide him across the polished floor. She managed to drag him through the branching corridor into one of the living quarters.

She was coming out the side corridor, wiping her

palms on her pants, when Kad appeared. "Luz! What are you doing here? Where's Marl?"

"Tasm ordered him to disengage the shield. I'm to brief you." Luz moved a few steps closer. "We're taking the archway."

"But it's too soon," Kad protested.

Luz moved closer, lowering her voice. "We're only taking the cylindrical unit. It's the key component."

Kad looked at her, startled. "That's true . . . the arch is just a solid neutronium ring that carries the magnetic resonances."

"That's what I thought." With one quick motion, she jabbed the hypospray against Kad's neck and emptied it.

Kad was smaller than Marl. He went so rigid that his back arched. Something gurgled in his throat, and he turned an alarming shade of blue.

Luz reached out to try to soften his fall. For a moment she was shaken out of her resolve. Kad's eyes were open and staring, and his entire body shook.

Then she remembered the birthing world. If she didn't act now and carry through with her engagement, the portal would be lost to the Petraw. Her goal was too important for her to hesitate now. Her people needed the interstellar transporter technology.

Uhura tried hailing the Klingons again on all channels, thinking they were breaking off their attack and finally ready to open discussions. But there was nothing. "No answer to our hails, sir."

"No," Kirk agreed. "Something's not right."

The bridge officers shifted uneasily. Many were glancing from their panels to the screen, where the Klingon battleships hung motionless yet menacing.

That's when the Kalandan's subspace channel was activated. Uhura said, "Sir! Commander Tasm is hailing us."

"I can't wait to hear this," Kirk muttered. "On screen."

Uhura opened the channel, routing it directly to the screen. Commander Tasm appeared, replacing the silent Klingon vessels, her head and shoulders filling the large screen. Her expression was closer to blank than serene. This time, Uhura thought her particolored eyelids seemed too festive and expressive for her face.

"Captain Kirk, we've been tricked. One of my officers has planted a tractor-projector on the planetoid. That unit is creating the illusion of the three Klingon vessels."

"A member of your own crew did it," Kirk said with deceptive quiet. "And you didn't know about it?"

"Officer Luz." Tasm frowned. *"She's been acting strangely since we discovered the station. It appears she's down there now, in spite of my orders."*

"She's inside the station?" Kirk demanded.

"Our sensors don't read her on the surface," Tasm confirmed.

"Drop the shield," Kirk ordered.

While Tasm worked on the screen, Uhura prepared to hail Mr. Spock. The Kalandan shield was much stronger than Scotty's, and they couldn't get a subspace message through the interference. Just as Uhura finished keying in the proper sequence, an indicator light flashed in one of the open frequencies, then was gone. Some kind of communications blip.

Uhura was distracted when Kirk stood up and took

several steps forward. Tasm was working faster now, apparently having difficulty.

"Commander," he warned. "We're waiting."

Tasm looked up, more worried than Uhura had ever seen her. *"I can't drop the shield. Something's jammed it."*

Kirk's tone was biting. "Do you expect me to believe that?"

"Yes!" she exclaimed, staring at him. *"It's been tampered with. Perhaps Luz did it from inside. . . ."*

Kirk's fist clenched. "We have to get inside that station."

Commander Kolar of the Klingon battleship *GhIj* whirled on her second officer, cuffing him so hard across the head that the man flew against the bulkhead. "I ordered communications silence!" Kolar roared.

The other Klingon officers shifted at their stations, growling low in their throats. The second officer hurriedly got to his feet and resumed his station, even though he knew that he might get cuffed again.

Commander Kolar raised her gloved hand, but didn't bother to follow through when the officer didn't flinch. He offered no excuses, either, for contacting the *Leng,* the battleship that accompanied them. If he had, he would be dead and another would rise to fill his place.

Kolar swung back into her command chair under the heavy main bulkheads. The *GhIj* was a fortress, ready to destroy those who dared to strike at the Klingon Empire.

"Status," Kolar demanded.

"Captain! Nearing the last known coordinates of the

defense cruiser *'Ong*. We will be within sensor range in four *tup*."

"And the *Leng?*" That was the other battleship. Kolar was the superior commander of the sortie. This territory belonged to neither the Federation nor the Klingons. Her actions could be the start of a Klingon expansion into these sectors.

Her orders were to investigate the distress signal sent by the *'Ong*. There was no explanation for why the cruiser had deviated so far from its normal patrol, nor why it had been engaged in battle with a Starfleet vessel.

Kolar didn't care why. She liked surprises. They made the battle all the more juicy. And with two battleships at her command, she could lay waste to anything that tried to stop them.

Chapter Eighteen

"WE'RE BREACHING that shield, Commander!" Captain Kirk insisted. "There must be some weakness in it."

"It bonds atomically to the bedrock," Tasm explained. *"The frequencies are overlapping, so there's no gap in the cycle. A quantum torpedo might destroy it, but the shock wave would kill everyone inside."*

Kirk turned away, thinking hard. Both Scotty and Spock, the two men who might know a way around that shield, were trapped inside the station. And he had a feeling that time was slipping away from them.

They couldn't use the phasers to punch through the bedrock because of the layers of diburnium-osmium alloy protecting the outpost below. If the phasers were set high enough to pierce the alloy, it would impact disastrously against the forcefield layers.

"What about a low-level phaser beam?" Kirk wondered to himself.

"Sir?" Sulu asked, looking back questioningly.

"The entrance chamber has rock ceilings. It's only partially below the surface."

On screen, Commander Tasm was also watching him. *"But the Teleris shield is over that chamber."*

"Yes, but we can bounce a low-level phaser blast off the diburnium-osmium alloy so it angles up *underneath* the shield."

"Cut a new door into the place," Sulu agreed.

Kirk hit the intercom to give general orders, "Engineering, reconfigure the phasers for drilling. Momita, get the deflection angle. How much power will we need?"

While his crew dealt with the task at hand, Kirk watched Tasm. "We're going in whether you like it or not."

"I'll meet you on the surface," she assured him, closing the channel.

Sidling up to the corridor that led from the command center down to the portal chamber, Luz could hear the echo of voices. It was difficult to understand the words because of the sound-absorbing walls.

Pitching her voice to Kad's clipped tones, she called out, "Mr. Scott, please help me with Marl."

The voices grew louder, and she withdrew around the edge of the doorway. The hypospray was ready, aimed at the spot where she would lunge at him. She didn't care if it went into his arm or his back—better that than to miss entirely.

Footsteps echoed down the corridor. It could be both men. She desperately hoped it wasn't both of them.

The officer in the red tunic stepped over the threshold. "Lad, where are ye?" he called out.

Luz jabbed the hypospray into his shoulder and unloaded it into him. Scott staggered away, his eyes wide. Stuttering, his cry to warn his fellow officer was incoherent.

Luz darted in and grabbed his phaser from his belt. Ripping it off its holster, she aimed it at Scott. One of his hands went out as he started to fall.

Her finger pressed the button and a beam of pure light shot out and hit him squarely in the chest. His body flew back and hit the floor, sliding in an untidy heap.

Luz leaped for the wall next to the doorway, aiming the phaser across it. Three down and one to go. The hardest one of all. The Vulcan, with his superior hearing, was probably aware that something was going on.

Scott was far over to one side. Spock would have to come right to the door to see him.

There was nothing. No sound. She was sweating under the unusual amount of hair required by the Kalandan disguise. But she didn't make a sound, even her breathing remained perfectly silent.

She wasn't sure if Spock was coming or not, but her instincts told her to wait. He must have heard Scott's strangled cry. Or the high whine of the phaser in the doorway.

She saw him first. Her finger tightened on the phaser and caught him sideways. Spock spun, but the power was too high for him to resist.

She fired again, for longer this time, as long as he was standing.

The Vulcan fell in the doorway, his own phaser dropping from his hand. She waited a moment to be sure he was down, but his sudden pallor showed the effects of the prolonged phaser blast.

Stepping over his legs, Luz ran down the corridor. So close, she was so close to getting her longed-for reward.

Engineering was ready as soon as the computer supplied the calculations setting power and angle of impact. It was timed to match with their position over the planetoid.

"Entering range," Sulu reported.

"Fire phaser banks." Kirk sat forward to watch the screen as the low-level beam shot down at the planetoid.

The illusion of a Class-M atmosphere churned at the point of entry. Soon a dark cloud trailed away from the phaser beam as the planetoid rotated, carrying the debris with it.

Finally the phaser beam shut off. "Operation complete," Sulu reported.

Kirk nodded shortly, getting up. "Mr. Sulu, you have the bridge. I'm going down."

Sulu nodded sharply. "Aye, sir!"

Kirk paused at the top of the stairs. "If I don't signal or drop the shield in five minutes, send down a full security team."

"Aye, sir," Sulu said more grimly. He waited until Kirk left the bridge before taking his seat.

Luz was glad to see that the archway appeared unharmed by their efforts to dismantle it from the station. Truly, it was a waste of effort to salvage the arch.

Rushing to the subprocessor, Luz let out a frustrated exclamation. The power had been shut off. It would take time for the subprocessor to cycle back on.

Determined, Luz powered up the computer. Then she activated the anti-grav units on either side. The unit rose with a humming sound.

She leaned against the subprocessor to push it closer to the archway. Abruptly, the monofilament cable extended to its maximum length and stopped. She was less than an arm's length away from the arch. But if she cut the monofilament, that would sever the link to the arch that provided the proper resonance.

She deactivated the anti-grav units. Apparently there was a minor flaw in her plan. She would have to leave the processor behind and take just the blue neutronium cylinder.

Luz grabbed the maser-saw and held it in one hand. She would have to cut through the monofilaments leading to the cylinder while she was inside the arch. Surely there was a fail-safe delay that would keep her from losing an arm or her head. Scientists as smart as the Kalandans would not ignore such a basic technological rule.

The subprocessor had a few crons to go before it cycled onto full power, but the shield would buy her the time she needed to get away.

She was already thinking about her beloved birthing world. How could she think of anything else? She could almost see the smooth oval chambers, warm and soft to the touch. The glow that shone from every surface. And the matriarchs themselves in the magnificent birthing chamber.

Luz could hardly wait to return with the interstellar transporter. Nothing would ever be the same again.

Kirk accepted a fully charged phaser from the transporter chief. As he took position, he briefly considered waiting for the security detail to arrive. But Tasm wasn't a threat to him. She also wouldn't bother to wait for him now that the station had been breached.

Kirk materialized on the planetoid, coughing a bit from the dust still hanging in the air. Slowly the yellow haze settled and he could see the gaping, blackened hole torn through the rock-strewn surface. It appeared to point directly at the large butte that was protected by the shield.

Tasm was at the edge of the gash, looking down inside. "It may have worked."

With that, she jumped lightly into the phaser trench.

Kirk stuck his phaser onto the back of his belt, and leaped down after her. The rock was melted smooth on the sides, but the top had partially caved in, leaving gaping holes in the roof and piles of rubble on the floor. As they made their way through the tunnel, Kirk reached up one hand to balance himself against the jutting rocks in the ceiling. It felt warm and fairly stable.

They emerged at the top of the wall inside the entrance chamber. It had been ripped apart by the phaser beam. The computer node in the ceiling was vaporized, as was the lift Spock had used. The walls were peeling long ribbons of plasticized osmium.

Tasm made a low expression of satisfaction and dropped down into the chamber. Kirk followed as soon as she got out of the way.

He pulled his communicator out. "Report, Mr. Spock. Scotty, come in." After a few moments, he urgently repeated, "Spock, report!"

Tasm shook her head over her padd, quickly folding it back up and shoving it into her pouch. "My officers haven't accessed the feed yet."

Kirk took one look at her face, and knew he wasn't going to waste time deactivating the shield. Security would follow them down.

Kirk ran through the corridor with Tasm close behind. They slid through the nexus chambers, breaking into a sprint in the long corridors.

Then Kirk saw Scotty lying in the command center. The captain's heart was pounding as he raced toward his friend.

He stopped short at the sight of Spock, lying stunned across the doorway leading to the portal chamber.

Kirk wanted nothing more than to drop down to his knees and see if they were still alive, but the floor began to move as a strong tremor shook the station. Light flashed from the corridor leading to the chamber where the portal lay unprotected.

"The portal!" Tasm cried out.

Kirk sprinted down the corridor and swung through the door, rounding the computer bank.

Luz was half-buried in the brilliant flashing discharge set off between the dimensions. She was leaning forward, a maser-saw poised over the monofilaments connecting the cylindrical unit to the Starfleet subprocessor.

On the other side of the portal was an unimaginable vista, as if Luz stood just inside an enormous crevice that sank hundreds of kilometers into the planetary crust. On top, the windblown sand piled high against the sides of two metal-plated structures. The lurid orange sky was nearly filled by a large sun looming over the horizon.

"No!" Tasm cried out behind Kirk. Her momentum carried her forward, knocking into him.

Kirk lurched toward the portal, as Tasm tackled Luz. He stopped himself with one hand against the arch, giving his entire body a shock. Tasm wrestled with Luz as the monofilaments from the cylinder stretched.

The tremor grew stronger, nearly shaking him off his feet.

Kirk couldn't let them get away with the interstellar transporter. In a split-second decision, he dived through the portal as they fell through.

The flashing light blinded his eyes and the Kalandan chamber disappeared.

Chapter Nineteen

SINCE THE STATION had almost killed Sulu twice, he had a healthy respect for its capabilities. His eyes were fastened on the chronometer, watching the seconds tick down.

Sulu pressed the intercom to transporter room four. "Security team ready to beam down?"

But instead of a female voice, Dr. McCoy came on. *"We're in position."*

"Dr. McCoy!" Sulu said in surprise.

"You may need a doctor down there," McCoy said by way of explanation.

Sulu reflexively rubbed his shoulder. Only in the last day had the stiffness gone out of it. Last night he had woken in a shaking sweat, reliving those awful minutes as he and Reinhart were choked into unconsciousness.

The shield was still holding and only one minute was left of Kirk's original five.

"Prepare to transport," Sulu ordered.

Lt. Uhura turned in her chair. "Lieutenant, we're receiving a hail from the Kalandan ship."

Not now! Sulu thought. But he said, "On screen." It was the other female Kalandan officer. *"Officer Mlan here. Have you heard from your captain?"*

"Negative," Sulu said warily. He didn't like the way the Kalandans stood so close to the screen. It seemed like an intimidation tactic.

Officer Mlan glanced down at her panel. *"Neither have we. We've detected two Klingon vessels approaching."*

Sulu let his lip raise in contempt. "Apparently making Klingon ships appear out of nowhere is your specialty."

He turned and made a motion for Uhura to cut transmission.

Momita reported, "Sir, I do have two Klingon battleships on long-range sensors."

"Déjà vu," Sulu muttered. He waited until the Kalandan was gone and the screen showed the planetoid again. Lt. Radha was seated at his usual station, so he told her, "Target the locations of the energy emissions, Radha."

"Aye, sir," Radha acknowledged.

The whine of the phaser banks echoed subtly through the bridge. Even in his quarters, Sulu could always tell when phasers were being fired.

On screen, the three Klingon ships that appeared poised half a million kilometers away blinked out of existence. "They're gone," Chekov said.

Sulu checked the screen on the arm of the command chair. The illusions were gone, but the Klingon vessels they had just detected on long-range sensors were still there.

"Sir!" Momita exclaimed. "Two Klingon battleships approaching at bearing six-zero mark four."

Sulu hit the intercom to the transporter. "Dr. McCoy, get down there and find out what's happening. There's two Klingon battleships approaching!"

Before the words were out of his mouth, the *Enterprise* lurched to one side. Sulu was nearly flung out of the chair. The ship heaved under him once again, then settled.

The red-alert lights were flashing automatically as the inertial dampers compensated. Sulu pushed himself up straight, calling out, "What was that?"

Science Officer Momita staggered back to her station, staring into the sensor hood. "A power surge from the station!"

Sulu remembered the way the power readings had redlined on his tricorder as the *Enterprise* was transported one thousand light-years away.

He hit the intercom. "Transporter room four!"

After a pause, McCoy answered again. *"We're here. A bit shaken up, but ready to go."*

"Losira's on the loose again," Sulu told McCoy, knowing he would understand the reference. "Better get down there fast!"

Dr. McCoy was surrounded by guards in red uniforms. They swarmed over the edge of the phaser burn and clambered through the deflection tunnel into the station. McCoy appreciated their presence, remembering how efficiently the defense computer had killed D'Amato.

Reinhart was in charge of the security team, as he was the most familiar with the station. He directed the guards down the corridor. A male and female Argelian, both with long hair tied back in flowing tails, moved swiftly just behind Reinhart, who took the lead. Other guards used their tricorders to instantly search the botany labs for life-forms—dead or alive.

McCoy kept starting at sounds, thinking that Losira would suddenly appear, ready to murder them.

They found the first unconscious body in one of the living quarters. But before McCoy could examine the Kalandan, he was called to help Scotty.

In the command center, Scotty was just groggily sitting up. "What happened?" McCoy demanded, whipping out his medical scanner. "Phaser stun, level two. You're not going to feel so great tonight."

Scotty was fumbling at his belt. "She took it from me! Th' Kalandan doctor."

McCoy felt a sinking in his stomach. "Are you sure it was Luz?"

"I'm as sure as I'm sitting here, Doctor!"

McCoy didn't want to believe it.

Guards called out from the living quarters as they carried the two male Kalandans out. Both were unconscious and looked blue rather than yellowish. McCoy rapidly scanned them. "They've been given an overdose of the sporophyte antidote."

"She must have gotten to them first," Scotty said, groaning as he rubbed his shoulder. "I think she got me with th' hypospray, too. But I was about ready fer another booster."

McCoy was already heading for the corridor to the portal, looking for Captain Kirk. They had scanned everywhere else.

But only Spock was leaning over the subprocessor.

The portal itself was quiet, but there was a residual hum in the room, as if the plasticized osmium had absorbed a tremendous amount of power.

"Spock! Where's Captain Kirk?" McCoy demanded.

"The captain?" It was the closest to being startled he had ever seen Spock.

Scotty came up behind them. "What're ye talking about, Doctor? Isn't th' captain on board th' *Enterprise?*"

"No, he beamed down first to find you!" McCoy's eyes widened at the sight of the portal. "Did he . . . go through that thing?"

Spock clasped his hands behind his back. "If you will look closely, you will see that the main component of the portal is missing."

McCoy moved forward, seeing for the first time the stretched and ragged ends of monofilament hanging out the hole in the side of the subprocessor. The cylindrical unit was gone.

"It's ruined!" Scotty exclaimed, fingering the monofilaments. "Without th' cylinder, there's no way to open th' portal."

"This is how I discovered the unit," Spock explained. "The portal has recently been activated. I am awaiting a self-diagnostic of the subprocessing unit."

"Who else is missing?" McCoy demanded. "Commander Tasm was with Kirk. And what happened to Luz?"

"She stunned me with Mr. Scott's phaser." McCoy thought he could see a wince of stun-shock in Spock's face. Even a Vulcan could only take so much, and Spock had been working around the clock for days.

"Could all three go through the portal at once?" McCoy asked.

"Theoretically, it would take less power than re-motely transporting the *Enterprise*," Spock confirmed.

"There was a tremendous quake just before we beamed down. It shook the whole ship."

"But why?" Scotty demanded. "Why would th' captain leave without telling us where he was goin'?"

"Perhaps he didn't have any choice," McCoy said darkly.

Spock was the only one who wasn't looking perturbed. The stoic security guards were exchanging troubled looks.

"We've got to get th' captain back!" Scott exclaimed.

"That will be difficult without the prime component," Spock pointed out.

McCoy exchanged an outraged look with Scotty before turning on Spock. "Don't you get it, Mr. Spock? The captain may have been taken by force!"

"Doctor, I will ask you to refrain from speculation. The portal will tell us the truth momentarily."

Before McCoy could protest Spock's cold-blooded attitude, the subprocessor beeped. Spock consulted the panel. "A resonance echo will appear revealing the last function the portal performed."

The mist began to form in the portal. Spock's tricorder was on and aimed at it.

The image was faint and hazy, but McCoy squinted to make out the incredible view of towering cliffs plunging straight into the ground beneath a tangerine sky. But the foreground held his attention. There was a silhouette of two slender humanoids grappling with each other in one corner of the portal. The cylindrical unit was raised between them.

"There's Jim!" McCoy pointed to the silhouette next

to the battling couple. It looked like Kirk was jumping through the portal.

After a few moments, the mist faded and the distortion gradually eased as the image disappeared.

"It appears the captain went voluntarily," Spock commented.

"But why?" McCoy insisted. "Do you recognize that place?"

"Negative, Doctor." Turning off the tricorder, he slung it over his shoulder. "I will compare it with the computer database on board the *Enterprise*."

Spock neatly attached the anti-grav units to the subprocessor to transport it back to the ship.

"Can't that thing tell us where they went?" McCoy asked, sticking to practicalities. The *Enterprise* could just go fetch Jim.

Spock looked thoughtfully at the subprocessor. "I will have to run a full diagnostic with the ship's computer."

"We don't have much time." McCoy realized he hadn't updated Spock on their current situation. With the captain missing, Spock was now officially in command. "Two Klingon battleships were detected on long-range sensors just before we beamed down."

Spock appeared to be computing the time they had left, then made his decision. "Reinhart, make sure everyone evacuates the station."

Reinhart gave the orders, and the guards immediately began a level-three scan as they withdrew, to make sure there was no one left inside this time.

"What about the Kalandans?" McCoy demanded.

Spock input commands into the anti-grav units. The units ticked and the subprocessor rose to knee-height. "The other Kalandans are free to go."

"Go? What about the station?"

"There will no longer be a station."

McCoy couldn't believe his ears. "What're you going to do, Spock?"

Spock picked up Scotty's phaser from where Luz had dropped it. "The station must be destroyed."

"Are you mad!" McCoy exclaimed, as Scotty also expressed his surprise.

Spock was apparently unconcerned about their reaction. "We do not know what other technological wonders this station may contain. We cannot allow the Klingons to take possession of it."

McCoy felt a rising panic. "You can't destroy this station, Spock! What about the captain?"

"The captain is no longer here, doctor. And our orders are clear."

"Aye," Scott reluctantly agreed. "We're not to let th' station fall into Klingon hands. But we *can* fight for her, Mr. Spock!"

Spock made some adjustments to the phaser. "Our tactical position is not sufficient to defeat two Klingon battleships."

"But what about the Kalandans?" Scotty demanded. "They'll fight with us!"

"Will they, Mr. Scott? May I remind you that they have lost their commander, and two of their top officers are incapacitated. If they do fight, I estimate a seventy-eight-percent probability that they will destroy the *Enterprise* in order to retain possession of the station." Spock went over to a gaping hole in the flooring.

"What are you doing, man?"

The Vulcan kneeled down next to the hole. "Mr.

Scott discovered an access point to the forcefield layers of this station. It is part of the magnetic field generator."

McCoy watched in morbid fascination as Spock unsealed the edges of a sheet of thick alloy. The Vulcan carefully removed it from the hole.

An electric-blue radiance filled the air over the open conduit, creating such a brilliant shine that McCoy's eyes narrowed. There was a lot of energy humming through there.

Spock appeared to be unaffected by the dangerous spectacle. "As Officer Marl nearly discovered, an energy discharge of sufficient power at this point could disintegrate this part of the station."

"Vulcan ears hear everythin'," Scotty was muttering under his breath.

"This isn't right," McCoy exclaimed. "We can't—I can't let you . . . We can't let him do it!"

Spock calmly interjected, "I am in command, Dr. McCoy."

McCoy stared at him, aghast. It couldn't be right! But he never won when he argued against Spock. He had logic on his side, much as McCoy didn't want to admit it. Still, it felt wrong.

"Yes, Mr. Spock," he finally said, seeing that he was waiting for an answer. "You are in command."

"Then proceed with your orders." Spock checked with the security guards to find that the station had been completely evacuated except for the three of them. Fair warning was given to the Kalandans of what they were about to do. They didn't respond.

Spock set the phaser in the hole, balancing it next to the open forcefield layer. "Gentlemen, we have five minutes before the phaser overloads and disrupts the forcefield layer."

It was a blur to McCoy, getting out of the Kalandan station. He only knew he didn't want to leave the place. It was their last link to Jim. But the captain was gone, and Spock was relentless.

After they beamed up, McCoy rushed to the screen in the transporter room to view the planetoid. Spock was already giving Sulu orders to plot a course away from the Kalandan station.

McCoy stared at the blue and brown sphere. Unlike most planets, this one had no shadow, because there was no sun. It made it seem like a toy planetoid, something that wasn't real.

As it grew smaller, everyone felt it. They were leaving the captain behind, abandoning him.

"The Klingons won't stay to search a science station," McCoy exclaimed. "They have no reason to think the planetoid is anything special. We could come back to look for him."

Spock joined McCoy at the screen, gazing at the planetoid. "Captain Kirk is no longer on the Kalandan station, Doctor. We must look for him elsewhere."

Something expanded at the curve of the planetoid, then blossomed into an explosion.

"There she goes!" Scotty exclaimed in regret.

Jim can't be there! McCoy thought wildly. His mind knew the captain had transported light-years away, but he couldn't help feeling that the captain was still on the station.

The planetoid receded quickly, obscuring the signs of destruction. Spock ordered the *Enterprise* to warp four, and it instantly became a dot on the screen. McCoy continued to stare at it, fervently wishing he didn't feel as if Jim was somehow trapped inside that arch. Which was now buried under tons of debris.

The others drifted out of the transporter room. Everyone was subdued.

McCoy stayed looking at the stars on the screen. Captain Kirk had to be out there. Among all those stars, where was he now?

POCKET BOOKS
PROUDLY PRESENTS

SIR APROPOS OF NOTHING

PETER DAVID

Available from
Pocket Books Hardcover

Turn the page for a preview of
Sir Apropos of Nothing. . . .

As I stood there with the sword in my hand, the blade dripping blood on the floor, I couldn't help but wonder if the blood belonged to my father.

The entire thing had happened so quickly that I wasn't quite sure how to react. Part of me wanted to laugh, but most of me fairly cringed at what had just occurred. I didn't do particularly well with blood. This tended to be something of a hardship for one endeavoring to become a knight, dedicated to serving good King Runcible of Isteria, a ruler who more often than not had his heart in the right place.

The recently slain knight also had his heart in the right place. This had turned out to be something of an inconvenience for him. After all, if his heart had been in the wrong place, then the sword wouldn't have pierced it through, he wouldn't be dead, and I wouldn't have been in such a fix.

I stood there stupidly in the middle of Granitz's chambers. Like much of the rest of the castle, it was somewhat chilly . . . all the more so because I was only partly dressed and the sweat on my bare skin was feeling unconscionably clammy. There were long, elegant candles illuminating the room, giving it a rosy glow, since thick drapes had been drawn over the large windows to keep out both daylight and prying eyes. From nearby on the large and damaged four-poster bed, my lover—and the knight's wife (well, widow)—was letting out short gasps, trying to pull air into her lungs and only marginally succeeding. The tiled floor seemed to tilt under me for a moment, and I steadied myself as my mind raced, trying to determine what the hell I was going to do next.

The knight's name had been Sir Granitz of the Ebony Swamps, although he was generally referred to as "Sir Granite." The nickname had been well earned, for on the battlefield he had been indeed a sight to see. I had seen it myself, many a time . . . from a safe distance, of course, since my mother, God bless her, had not raised an idiot for a son. Understand: I did not, nor have I ever, shrunk from a fight when it was absolutely necessary. However, my definition of "absolutely necessary" wasn't precisely in keeping with that of everyone else in my immediate sphere.

For people like Granite, "absolutely necessary" included times of war, matters of honor, and similar esoterica. For me, the term "absolutely necessary" meant "self-defense." I considered war to be an utter waste of my time and energy, since most wars involved people I did not know arguing over matters I did not care about in pursuit of goals that would not have any direct impact upon me. As for honor, that was an ephemeral consideration. Honor did not feed, clothe, or protect me, and seemed to exist primarily to get otherwise inoffensive creatures into a world of trouble.

"Self-defense," however, was a consideration that I could easily comprehend. Whether it be an envious knight attacking me on horseback, an enraged dragon belching plumes of flame, or a squadron of berserker trolls swarming over the ramparts of a castle, those were instances where my own neck was at stake and I would happily hack and slash as the situation required so that I might live to see another sunrise.

I liked sunrises. They made anything seem possible.

Now, Granite . . . he was the type who would fight anywhere, anytime, at the least provocation. That is precisely the kind of attitude that gets one killed at a young age if one is not a formidable fighter. To his credit, that certainly described Granite. Well over six feet tall and built like a brick outhouse, he often found it necessary to enter a room sideways, his shoulders being too broad to be accommodated by a standard doorframe.

Sir Granite had returned most unexpectedly, at a moment that could best be described as inopportune. For at that particular point in time, I had been in the middle of opportuning myself of his wife.

As burly, as brusque, as fearsome as Granite had been, the Lady Rosalie had been the opposite. Delicate and pale, Rosalie had cast an eye that clearly fancied me in my direction. Considering that, at the time she did it, I was mucking out the stables and up to my elbows in horse manure, she clearly saw something within me not readily apparent from my surface appearance. She and old Granite had just come in from a ride; he perched upon his white charger, and she riding daintily sideways on a brown mare. She winked at me and I hurriedly wiped my hands on the nearest cloth, aware of the disheveled and frankly tatty sight I must have presented. The Lady Rosalie chose that moment to try and dismount. But her foot snagged on the stirrup and she tumbled forward, only my quick intervention preventing her from hitting the straw-covered floor. I caught her, amazed by how light she was. I'd bounced soap bubbles off my fingertips that had more substance.

For the briefest of moments, Rosalie insinuated her body against mine, mashing her breasts against my stained tunic. They were round and felt surprisingly firm beneath her riding clothes. It was not the fall that had carried her against me in that manner; she had done it deliberately with a subtle arching of her back that only I detected. Then, after the ever-so-brief gesture, she stepped back and put her hand to her throat in a fluttery manner. "Thank you, squire," she said, her voice having a most alluring musical lilt.

"Not . . . a problem, milady," I replied.

Old Granite did not seem to be the least bit supportive of my chivalric endeavors. His thick red mustache bristled and he said contemptuously, "I give you lesson after lesson, Rosalie, and still you can't so much as get off the damned horse. You shouldn't have caught her, squire. A far greater favor you'd have done her if you'd let her fall flat on her ass. It's the only way she's going to learn anything about successful mounting."

"Well . . . one of two ways," I said in a low voice, just enough for her to hear. Her cheeks colored, but not in embarrassment because she put a hand to her mouth to stifle what clearly sounded like a giggle. I grinned at her. She did not return the smile with her mouth, but it was clearly reciprocated in her eyes.

Granite smoothly jumped off his horse and thudded to the ground like a boulder. "Come, madam," he said, sticking out an elbow in a manner intended to be gallant but that instead simply appeared stiff and uncomfortable. This was not a man who was accustomed to the slightest gesture of gentility. She took his elbow and walked out with him, but glanced back at me just before they left.

From that moment, it was simply a matter of time.

I knew all about Granite. He was typical of Runcible's knights, spouting words of chivalry and justice, but doing whatever he desired behind the king's back. He made polite and politic noises to the king, but he could be as much of a brute as any common highwayman or any member of the Thugs' Guild, and he also had a string of mistresses in various towns and villages. He frequented the whores' tent, which was usually set up at the outskirts of an encampment during a campaign. More than one tart had supposedly come away from the amorous encounter with bruises to show for it when Granite was impatient with his own . . . performance. The mighty knight, you see, had a bit more trouble wielding his sword off the battlefield than on, if you catch my drift, and that difficulty translated to welts for those who couldn't easily overcome his problems.

I, however, had no such difficulties.

The Lady Rosalie, "heeding" her husband's suggestions to improve her riding abilities, took to the stables more and more frequently to get in practice time. Well . . . allegedly, that was the reason. But an intended hour of riding would end up an hour of conversing with me as I groomed and tended to the horses while she laughed and giggled and watched me perform my duties with a sort of doe-eyed fascination. I knew exactly where matters were taking us, and did absolutely nothing to deter them in their course.

One day she asked me to accompany her on a jaunt, since her husband had gone to deal with a minor uprising in the nearby city of Pell, and she was concerned lest bandits be wandering the roads. This, of course, wasn't her major concern. We rode several miles away from the good king's stables, chatting about trivialities, nonsense, and just about everything except for what really occupied our thoughts. By the lakeside, on a cool morning, nature took its course.

Let us just say that she did not ride exclusively sidesaddle.

I'm sure that I provided little more than an amusement to her, a dalliance. The obvious conclusion was that she was using me to get back at her husband, to make him jealous. But I doubt that was the case, because siccing the green-eyed monster upon Granite could only have fatal consequences. Rosalie may not have been the most polished apple to fall off the tree, but she was most definitely not suicidal. Maintaining a shroud of secrecy over our relationship heightened the likelihood of her keeping her pretty head on her shoulders. Besides, when you get down to it, isn't it the very illicitness of an affair, the forbidden nature of it, which makes it so exciting? Even pedestrian sex can be elevated to new heights when one isn't supposed to be having it.

That was probably what kept it going. Old Granite had made very clear to all and sundry that he thought very little of his wife's mental prowess. He considered her something of a twit. But twit or not, she ably concealed the existence of her tawdry little escapades (and I say that with only the fondest of recollections and greatest esteem) from this great warrior who thought himself one of the most canny and discerning of men.

Consequently, when it all came crashing down, it landed with a most pronounced thud.

The Pell situation, which started as something rather inconsequential, began to spiral out of control. Granite made a tactical error, you see. There had been a hard core of individuals utterly opposed to pouring more tax money into the king's coffers. I couldn't blame them, really. Most of the money paid in taxes didn't go into providing resources for public works, but instead either lined the pockets of key knights, or served to fund foreign wars that most of the peasants never heard of and didn't care about.

The hard core of individuals were endeavoring to organize protests, even stonewall against further taxes. The other peasants were reluctant to join with them. This came as no surprise to me. Being a peasant, I know the mind-set. One becomes so used to being downtrodden that one starts to believe that it's nature's intent that one should inhabit a low rung in society. Lack of movement is a formidable force to overcome.

The rabble-rousers called themselves the Freedom Brigade and set themselves up as enemies of the king and his policies. But they weren't enemies, really. An enemy is someone who has the capability to do you genuine harm. Calling this lot enemies was like referring to head lice as criminal masterminds. They had the ability to irritate, but they were no threat. Only one of the "Brigadiers" had any knack for rabble-rousing at all. I knew him from the old days. His name was Tacit, he was damned good-looking, and the women tended to swoon when they saw him coming. But swoon-inducers aren't necessarily great leaders of men, because men tend to mistrust other men who are that handsome. They start thinking that there's some other agenda in force, such as seeking out leadership just to get the attention and favors of the women, and perhaps they're not wrong to believe that.

Besides, Tacit wasn't the leader of the Brigadiers anyway. I don't even recall the name of the leader offhand; that's how forgettable he was. He was simply stolid and determined to change things, and wasn't particularly good at making that happen.

The truth was, the Brigadiers really just wanted to be in the favorable position enjoyed by those they were opposing, which is usually the case of protesters. If Granite had given them just a taste of the good life, the Freedom Brigade would have melted like a virgin's protests on her wedding night. One of the best ways to dispose of enemies—even perceived ones such as the Brigadiers—is to make them over into allies and friends. When someone is not truly in a position to hurt you, that is the time to approach him or her with an air of camaraderie. Respect. Bribery. The Freedom Brigade could easily have been bought off. Hell, I suspect they could have been retooled into a formidable squad of tax collectors that would have put the king's own men to shame.

But not old Granite, oh no.

For Granite was a fighting man, you see. Put him on a field with a sword and buckler, give him a squadron behind him, point him in a direction—any direction—and say, "Kill," and watch him go at it. As a slaughtering machine, he was a thing of beauty. There was a tendency to elevate him in positions of importance and rank as a consequence. It's understandable, I suppose. Put yourself in the place of the king. You come riding up to a field after the battle is done, there are bodies strewn all over the place like clothes at a brothel, and there's one man standing there, wavering slightly, wearing tattered armor, copious amounts of blood (none of it his), and a somewhat demented smile. You would tend to think that this fellow knows what he's about. Such was the case with Granite.

Unfortunately, what the king did not realize is that just because one was skilled at one means of controlling an uprising—namely by whacking it until all of its internal organs are on the landscape—did not automatically translate into any sort of aptitude for handling other situations.

When Runcible learned of the situation in Pell, he sent Granite, convinced that he was dispatching one of his best men to attend to it. Were Pell in the midst of full-scale riot, Granite might indeed have been just the fellow for it. But matters were still controllable. Why wade in with a broadsword when a whispering dagger would do the job?

Well, Granite used a broadsword and a half. He and his men rode in like the great damned king's own Ninth Army, stampeded through Pell, rounded up a dozen townspeople at random and threatened them with beheading if they didn't produce the names of the Freedom Brigadiers. The citizenry, who were upset about their taxes but not *that* upset, coughed up the identities like phlegm. Better to live poor than die with a few extra coins in your pocket.

Granite then rounded up the Freedom Brigade. What a great bloody row. The noise, the screaming . . . it was horrific. They captured almost all of them, and—truth to tell—the Brigadiers didn't exactly conduct themselves as heroes. Playing at being freedom fighters, criticizing the king from a distance, declaring that taxes would not be forthcoming and that the king should take his best shot at collecting them—these are all well and good in the abstract. Faced with a sword to your throat, however, your priorities tend to shift. Rhetoric takes a second chair to saving your own skin. My understanding is that they begged, pleaded for their lives. They wept, they entreated, they soiled their breeches . . . in short, they made godawful fools of themselves.

Once again, Granite could have gotten out of the entire Pell mess with a minimum of fuss and muss. Not old blockhead, no. The unmanly wailing of the Brigadiers offended Granite's sensibilities. He felt that his valuable time had been wasted rounding up such clearly unworthy foes. This set his anger all a-bubbling, and he needed an outlet for his rage. As it turned out, the only available target was the Brigadiers.

So he put the stupid bastards to the sword, every one of them. Every one except Tacit. Tacit had not been captured with the rest. They tried to take him, to be sure. But when Granite made his sweep, which dragged in the rest, Tacit had managed to fight his way through it, battling with the ferocity of a manticore when faced with death. His freedom had not come without a price. He lost half an ear and his right eye, poor bastard. He took refuge in the Elderwoods, his old stomping grounds, which he and I frequented as children. Once he'd reached there, he was a phantom. There he healed, and eventually returned to Pell with an eyepatch and a new and deadly resolve. Tossed capriciously in the crucible, he'd come through it forged into a cold and formidable enemy.

He rallied the people of Pell in a way that no others of the Brigade had managed, and he turned the entire town into an army. Every man, woman, and child rallied behind him, refusing to pay taxes and demanding the head and private parts of Granite.

Granite obliged. He brought his head, his private parts, and his sword arm—all still connected to the rest of his sculpted body—and he also brought along armored troops. They laid siege to the town, and within hours all of Pell was aflame and easily sixty percent of the populace was dead, and another twenty percent or so was dying.

Naturally this resulted in an eighty percent drop in taxes from Pell, which was what all of the to-do was about in the first place. Granite, however, had lost sight of that.

King Runcible had not.

He didn't get truly angry—he rarely did. But he informed Granite that he was not happy, no, not happy at all with the situation. Granite hemmed, hawed, made apologies, and tried to defend the extreme actions he had taken. "We shall have to think on this," Runcible said finally, which is what he always said when faced with something unpleasant. He then ordered Granite to patrol the outer borders of the kingdom.

I was present when the order was given, standing discreetly behind Sir Umbrage of the Flaming Nether Regions, the elderly knight whom it was my "fortune" to be squiring at the time. It was easy to remain out of sight behind Umbrage. He was such an uninteresting bastard that no one glanced in his direction. He would just stand there, long, skinny, white-haired, and jowly beneath his scraggly beard, leaning on his sword and nodding as if he were paying attention to what was going on.

Granite bowed, nodded, and left immediately.

I, opportunistic little creep that I was, saw my chance to have yet another toss with the Lady Rosalie. I waited until I saw Granite ride away on that great charger of his, and then went straight to the chambers that he shared with his lady.

Rosalie, bless her heart, read my mind. She was lying there, naked and waiting. And she was holding her crystal ball.

Now, Rosalie had no knack for fortune-telling, but she fancied that she did. She obtained the large crystal from a woman purporting to be an oracle, and she would stare into the crystal ball for hours on end, trying to discern her future. Every so often she would make thoughtful pronouncements in a voice that I think she thought was great and profound. In point of fact, it just sounded like Rosalie talking oddly. I never paid any mind to it. It seemed a harmless enough diversion.

"Did you see me coming in that?" I asked teasingly.

She smiled in that odd way that she had, that made the edges of her eyes all crinkly. "In a manner of speaking," she said, and laid the crystal ball on the floor.

My tunic was off and my leggings were just descending below my knees when the door burst open. There was Granite, looking considerably larger than he had when he'd been riding off into the distance minutes before.

I caught only the briefest of glimpses, though, because the moment the door opened, I had already rolled off the bed, landing on the far side, out of view. I may not have had a good deal going for me, but my reactions had always been formidably quick. Long practice, I suppose in keeping one eye behind me at all times. I lay paralyzed on the floor. The door slamming back against the wall had covered the noise of my thudding to the ground, but I was concerned that any further movement on my part might attract his attention. Granite was a formidable warrior with a sense of hearing only marginally less sharp than his blade. I held my breath so that he didn't hear it rasping against my chest, but I was positive that he could nonetheless detect my heart slamming in my rib cage. In any event, I certainly didn't want to risk making scrabbling noises against the floor. That would tip him for sure.

Rosalie was not the brightest of things, but barely controlled panic gave wings to her moderately capable brain. Upon the door slamming open, she had automatically clutched the sheet under her chin, covering herself. "Milord!" she burst out. She certainly did not need to feign her surprise. "I . . . I . . ."

I practically heard the scowl in his voice. "What are you about?" he demanded.

"I . . . I . . ."

"Well?!"

She suddenly tossed the sheet aside, wisely letting it tumble atop me to further hide me, although—truth be told—I'm not entirely certain how effective a disguise it would have been, since piles of laundry do not generally tend to quiver in fear. "I was . . . waiting for you, milord!" she said, throwing her arms wide and no doubt looking rather enticing in her utter nudity. "Take me!"

I still held my breath, which, actually, was no great trick, because my chest was so constricted I couldn't exhale if I'd wanted to. My heart had also stopped beating, and I was fairly sure my brain was in the process of shutting down. I was hoping, praying, that Granite would go for the bait. If he did, and she distracted him sufficiently, I could creep out on hands and knees while they were going at it.

"Take you where?" demanded Granite, never one to pick up on a cue.

"Here! Now!"

He had to go for it. How could he resist? Certainly I couldn't have. Then again, I wasn't a knight, at least not yet. Knights were apparently made of sterner stuff. Either that or Granite was just too block-stupid to be distracted from something confusing to him. Apparently he'd gotten a thought into his head, and the damned thing wouldn't be easily dislodged, probably because it was fairly quiet in his brain otherwise and the thought enjoyed the solitude.

"How could you have been expecting me when I didn't know I was coming back?" demanded Granite.

"I . . ." I heard her lick her lips, which were probably bone dry by that point. "I . . . anticipated . . . or hoped, at least . . . that you would return to service me once more before you left."

"I didn't. I came back to get my lucky dagger. I forgot it."

"Oh."

If Rosalie had just let that harmless little "Oh" sit there, we might well have avoided discovery. He was, after all, perfectly willing to accept that she was a nitwit. Unfortunately, because a silence ensued, Rosalie felt the need to fill it with words. "Yes. I . . . saw it over there on the wall and knew you'd be back."

Granite, unfortunately for us, was able to track the conversation. "You just said that you were hoping I'd return to service you. Now you say you knew I'd be back for the dagger."

"Yes, I . . . that is to say . . . I . . . that . . ."

There was another dead silence, and I could only imagine the blood draining from her face as her poor brain twisted itself about in confusion. I heard the door bang suddenly and prayed that he had simply exited with no further words . . . but that hope was short-lived as I heard the bolt slam into place.

Granite was no idiot. I had to give him that much. "What," I heard him rumble, "is going on?"

I thought furiously at her, as if I could project words into her brain in hopes that they would spill out of her mouth. *I am . . . tongue-tied by your presence, milord . . . I would say anything just in hopes of saying something you want to hear, milord . . . I hoped that, in your returning for your dagger, you would savage me like a wild animal, milord . . .*

Something. Anything.

"Don't . . ." There was a choked sob. "Don't hurt him, milord. . . ."

Anything but that.

I heard a roar then. I think the word *"What?!"* was in there somewhere, but it was like trying to sort out one particular scream from the howling of a hurricane. There was a quick sound of steps coming around the bed, and suddenly the sheet was yanked off me. My bare ass was still hanging out as I squinted up at Granite.

He wasn't moving. He trembled in place, seized with such fury that he could not yet budge.

I rolled to my feet, yanking my breeches up as I went. The bed was a huge four-poster affair, and I leaned against one of the thick oak bedposts, trying to compensate for my fairly useless right leg. I must have been quite the sight at that moment. At that age, I was thin and gawky. My arms were well muscled from years of hauling myself around while compensating for the lameness of my leg. My ears stuck out too much, and I didn't have normal hair so much as a thick, wild mane of red that proved annoyingly difficult to brush or style. My nose was crooked from the times in the past that it'd been broken. My best feature remained my eyes, which were a superb shade of gray, providing me with a grim and thoughtful look whenever I put my mind to it. However, I suspect at that point that he wasn't exactly concerned with admiring my orbs.

We stood there, frozen in time for half an ice age it seemed. I don't even think he quite focused on me at first, as if his brain was so overheated that he needed time to fully process the information. "I . . . know you!" he said at last. "You're Umbrage's squire! You clean out stables! You're Appletoe!"

"Apropos," I corrected him, and then mentally kicked myself. As if I wasn't in enough of a fix, I had to go and remind him of my name. Why didn't I just stick my neck out and offer to hack it through for him?

Then I realized he wasn't waiting for an invitation, as I heard the sword being drawn before I actually saw it. I took a step back, making sure to play up my limp so that I could seem as pathetic as possible.

His eyes were fixed on me, but he was clearly addressing his nude wife. "A squire? You cuckold me . . . for a squire? For a shoveler of horse manure? *For this you shame me?!*"

Rosalie was not going to be of any help. Her mouth was moving, but no sounds were coming out.

There was no point denying the actual cuckolding. I can be a dazzling liar given the right circumstances, but these were certainly not they. So I felt my only hope was to try and address the other side of the equation. "Now . . . now t . . . t . . . technically, mi . . .

milord," I stammered out, "there's been no, uh, actual shaming, as it were. No one knows. You, Rosalie, me . . . that is all. And if we can agree to, uh . . . keep this among ourselves, then perhaps we can just, well . . . forget this all happened, sweep it under the carpet until . . . until . . ."

I was going to say, "Until we're all dead and gone." Unfortunately, at that moment Rosalie found her voice.

"Until you leave again," she suggested.

He swung his sword around and bellowed like a wounded boar. I tried to back up. Not only did my limp impede me, but also my feet became tangled in the sheets and I tumbled to the floor. Rosalie let out a shriek.

I considered telling him at that point that he might or might not be my father, but that statement—albeit true enough—seemed to smack so much of a desperation move that I figured it would be perceived as a ploy. So I chose to appeal to the one thing which might serve as his weak spot.

"Where's the honor in this?!" I shouted.

He was standing directly over me, his sword drawn back and over his head, ready to bring it slamming down like a butcher slaughtering a bull. This was no ordinary sword, it should be noted. The damned thing had teeth: jagged edges running down either side, particularly useful for ripping and tearing. It was also formidable for a good old-fashioned slicing. If the blow had landed, it would have cleaved me from crotch to sternum. But he froze, his mustache bristling as if acquiring a life all its own. I thought for a moment that it was going to rip itself off his lip and come at me. "Honor?" he growled. "You have my wife . . . and speak to me of your honor?"

"Your honor, milord, not mine . . . I . . . I am nothing." I spoke as quickly as I could. "I am nothing, no one . . . but that, you see . . . that's the point . . ."

"What is?" The sword, which had a far more formidable point than any points in my repertoire, hadn't moved from its rather threatening position above me.

"Well, milord, obviously . . . when my corpse turns up, and you, as a man of honor, why, you'll have to own up to your slaying of me . . . and explain why . . ."

"I have no intention of hiding it," he snarled. "Not a man in the court will deny my right as a husband!"

"No question." I felt the longer I kept it going, the more chance

I had of talking him out of what was clearly his intended course. "But look at the slaughter situation."

"The . . . what?" The snarl had slightly vanished; he seemed a bit bemused.

"Look at you . . . full in your leathers, your sword in hand, rippling with power . . . and here I am, half-naked, on my back, unarmed . . . well, honestly!" I continued, as if scolding a recalcitrant child. I couldn't believe the tone of voice I was adopting. One would have thought that, in some fashion, I possessed the upper hand. "And a lowly, untitled squire with no land or privilege at that. Where is the challenge in skewering me? Where is the redemption of honor? A stain on your status as husband and man requires something more than mere butchery."

I would have felt just a bit better if the sword had wavered by so much as a centimeter. It did not. But neither did it come slamming down. "What," he asked, "did you have in mind?"

"A duel," I said quickly, not believing that I had managed to get it that far. "Tomorrow . . . you and me, facing off against one another in the proper manner. Oh, the outcome is foregone, I assure you. I'm but a squire, and lame of leg at that. You're . . . well . . . you're you . . ."

"That is very true," he said thoughtfully.

"Certainly you'll massacre me. But if we do it in the manner that I suggest, no one can look at you askance and say, 'So . . . you carved a helpless knave. Where is the challenge in that?'" I paused and then added boldly, "I'm right, milord. You know I am. A husband's honor restored. A philanderer put to rights in a way that no one can question. It is the thing to do."

I had him then. I knew that I did. I glanced at Rosalie, praying that she would keep her mouth shut and say nothing to spoil the moment. Thank the gods, her lips were tightly sealed.

In point of fact, I had no intention of battling Granite on the field of honor. The man could break a griffin in half. I wouldn't have had a chance against him; he would have driven my head so far down into my body that I would have been able to lace my boots with my teeth. Fighting him man to man would be suicide.

I intended to use the night between now and tomorrow to bundle together everything that I owned in the world—which was, admittedly, not much. Then, under cover of darkness, I would slip away. There was a wide world out there beyond the kingdom of Isteria, and I couldn't help but feel that there had to be sufficient room in it for Apropos. Granted, my flight would be an irretrievable besmirching of my honor. To hell with that. Honor did not pay bills, nor keep one warm at night. Apropos would disappear; I would take up a new identity. It wasn't as if the one that I had was all that wonderful anyway. Start a new life, learn a trade, perhaps become a knight eventually somewhere else. Who knew? Perhaps, at some point in the future, Granite and I would meet on the battlefield. We would face each other, glowering . . . and then, with any luck, I'd shoot him with an arrow from a safe distance.

All this occurred to me in a moment's time.

And then Granite said, "I don't care."

That was all the warning I had before the sword swung down toward me. . . .

Look for STAR TREK fiction from Pocket Books

Star Trek®: The Original Series

Star Trek: Deep Space Nine®

Star Trek: Voyager®

Star Trek®: New Frontier

Star Trek®: Starfleet Corps of Engineers (eBooks)

#1 • *The Belly of the Beast* • Dean Wesley Smith
#2 • *Fatal Error* • Keith R.A. DeCandido
#3 • *Hard Crash* • Christie Golden
#4 • *Interphase, Book One* • Dayton Ward & Kevin Dilmore
#5 • *Interphase, Book Two* • Dayton Ward & Kevin Dilmore
#6 • *Cold Fusion* • Keith R.A. Decandido
#7 • *Invincible, Book One* • Keith R.A. Decandido and David Mack
#8 • *Invincible, Book Two* • Keith R.A. Decandido and David Mack

Star Trek®: Invasion!

#1 • *First Strike* • Diane Carey
#2 • *The Soldiers of Fear* • Dean Wesley Smith & Kristine Kathryn Rusch
#3 • *Time's Enemy* • L.A. Graf
#4 • *The Final Fury* • Dafydd ab Hugh
Invasion! Omnibus • various

Star Trek®: Day of Honor

#1 • *Ancient Blood* • Diane Carey
#2 • *Armageddon Sky* • L.A. Graf
#3 • *Her Klingon Soul* • Michael Jan Friedman
#4 • *Treaty's Law* • Dean Wesley Smith & Kristine Kathryn Rusch
The Television Episode • Michael Jan Friedman
Day of Honor Omnibus • various

Star Trek®: The Captain's Table

#1 • *War Dragons* • L.A. Graf
#2 • *Dujonian's Hoard* • Michael Jan Friedman
#3 • *The Mist* • Dean Wesley Smith & Kristine Kathryn Rusch
#4 • *Fire Ship* • Diane Carey
#5 • *Once Burned* • Peter David
#6 • *Where Sea Meets Sky* • Jerry Oltion
The Captain's Table Omnibus • various

Star Trek®: The Dominion War

#1 • *Behind Enemy Lines* • John Vornholt
#2 • *Call to Arms...* • Diane Carey
#3 • *Tunnel Through the Stars* • John Vornholt
#4 • *...Sacrifice of Angels* • Diane Carey

Star Trek®: Section 31

    Rogue • Andy Mangels & Michael A. Martin
    Shadow • Dean Wesley Smith & Kristine Kathryn Rusch
    Cloak • S. D. Perry
    Abyss • Dean Weddle & Jeffrey Lang

Star Trek®: Gateways

#1 • *One Small Step* • Susan Wright
#2 • *Chainmail* • Diane Carey

Star Trek®: The Badlands

#1 • Susan Wright
#2 • Susan Wright

Star Trek®: Dark Passions

#1 • Susan Wright
#2 • Susan Wright

Star Trek® Omnibus Editions

    Invasion! Omnibus • various
    Day of Honor Omnibus • various
    The Captain's Table Omnibus • various
    Star Trek: Odyssey • William Shatner with Judith and Garfield Reeves-
      Stevens

Other Star Trek® Fiction

    Legends of the Ferengi • Ira Steven Behr & Robert Hewitt Wolfe
    Strange New Worlds, vols. I, II, III, and IV • Dean Wesley Smith, ed.
    Adventures in Time and Space • Mary P. Taylor
    Captain Proton: Defender of the Earth • D.W. "Prof" Smith
    New Worlds, New Civilizations • Michael Jan Friedman
    The Lives of Dax • Marco Palmieri, ed.
    The Klingon Hamlet • Wil'yam Shex'pir
    Enterprise Logs • Carol Greenburg, ed.

STAR TREK
SECTION 31

BASHIR
Never heard of it.

SLOAN
We keep a low profile....
We search out and identify
potential dangers to the
Federation.

BASHIR
And Starfleet sanctions
what you're doing?

SLOAN
We're an autonomous
department.

BASHIR
Authorized by whom?

SLOAN
Section Thirty-One was
part of the original
Starfleet Charter.

BASHIR
That was two hundred years
ago. Are you telling me
you've been on your own
ever since? Without specific
orders? Accountable to
nobody but yourselves?

SLOAN
You make it sound so
ominous.

BASHIR
Isn't it?

No law. No conscience. No stopping them.
A four book, all <u>Star Trek</u> series beginning in June.

Excerpt adapted from *Star Trek:Deep Space Nine*®
"Inquisition" written by Bradley Thompson & David Weddle.
2161